Praise for The Jaguar Prophecies by Phyllis Gunderson

I have read *The Jaguar Prophecies* by Phyllis Gunderson twice. It is not the typical 2012 cliché where thousands of cars and their screaming occupants tumble into yawning earthquake trenches, and half of Los Angeles sinks like a rock into the Pacific Ocean.

Jaguar Prophecies takes a more gentle, thoughtful, and even scientific approach to the event some people call Armageddon. Author Gunderson uses her story to point out how the earth experiences cycles, like those indicated in ancient Mayan and Chinese calendars, as the solar system passes through different parts of the galaxy where gravitational and magnetic forces change, shifting the earth's poles, and moving the equator. Sea levels change and tidal waves become huge as increased volcanic and earthquake activity shift the earth's crust. Volcanic dust in the atmosphere and fierce winds disrupt weather patterns and growing seasons. Geologists and astronomers say it has happened before, and Hopi and Mayan prophets say it will happen again.

Open-minded, thoughtful people who store food in sturdy homes at safe elevations will have an excellent chance of survival. Corrupt and unstable governments will disappear as the earth cleanses itself, a new birth at the threshold of a glorious new age. I applaud Gunderson for writing a novel to warn the world, while telling a delightful story, and providing an excellent bibliography for readers determined to know more and be better prepared.

—Lee Nelson

Doom and gloom? Not in this book. Phyllis Gunderson has written a warm, wise, and witty novel about one woman's search for the truth. When archaeologist Matt Howard is mistakenly invited to a Mayan festival in Mexico, she is marked and chosen to carry a message to the world. Matt's very human struggle to accomplish her purpose makes this book a standout amid the stories centered around the 2012 prophecies. Meticulously researched and lovingly written, *The Jaguar Prophecies* will leave you informed, in

—Elizabeth Lane

Enthralling!! Though it is a book of fiction, it is full of truth! I love the way it was written. It didn't drag or use a lot of useless or unnecessary words. I would highly recommend it! The author said what needed to be said, a warning was given, and those who have eyes to see and ears to hear will get the message and act upon it.

—Donna Max

The Jaguar Prophecies is a fantastic book! I couldn't put it down! Gunderson combines her vast understanding of archaeology, science, and ancient knowledge with wonderfully wacky characters and a fast-paced story to create a masterpiece.

—Katie Watkins

I liked the writing. It was descriptive and had terrific observations for the situations Matt found herself in, with creative and original insights that made the read fun and rewarding. While a novel, I enjoyed the brush with the archaeological, anthropological, historical, astrological, astronomical worlds. I hadn't read much about these topics before and am inspired to learn more. I highly recommend it.

—Greg Ford

In *The Jaguar Prophecies*, Phyllis Gunderson has combined the things I love in a book: page-turning anticipation and the opportunity to learn something in a fun, painless way. *The Jaguar Prophecies* was life-changing. No longer will I fear what might happen. Phyllis has inspired me to be prepared, to meet life without fear, and that's an accomplishment. Thank you, Phyllis! I am looking forward to reading more from this author.

—Elizabeth A. Firth

It gripped my attention right off and kept me reading all the way through to the last word. I appreciated that the science was skillfully interspersed in the story line so as not to bog me down with too many facts at any one time. That also made it so that I could actually retain more of the factual information. I also liked that the author didn't say the world was ending in 2012, as is the common belief among 2012ers. . . . I really enjoyed this book. I would definitely recommend it to neighbors and friends!

—Kassie Vance

Full of multiple sources of research wound tightly into a great story, with just the right touch of humanity and emotion mixed in. It's a single-sitting read.

—Kit Hooker

I love the way author Phyllis Gunderson uses a novel to bring together the warnings of astronomers, geologists, and Hopi prophets to explain why 2012 is the end date of ancient Mayan and Chinese calendars. Gunderson has convinced me that Mother Earth is entering a period of change that will impact every one of us. I read the entire book in one day, couldn't put it down. Phyllis Gunderson is now one of my favorite authors.

—Taylor Nielsen

Captivating, convincing, well-written—I was intrigued by the information.

—LeGrand L. Baker

Fascinating reading! The truth is pretty frightening sometimes, but I love that the heroine's humor shines through. Matt Howard is a great character. I hope there is more to come! The quote about telling the truth through a story was fantastic.

—Alice DeWitt

I loved Matt—what a great character. Phyllis Gunderson's book was really informative, and I learned so much.

—Maureen Stacey

Good things do come in small packages. *The Jaguar Prophecies* takes you on a trip and teaches you at the same time. Entertaining and hopeful!

—René Murdock

The story pulls you along to the point I found myself reading while cooking dinner, riding in the car, and following my husband around the house. It was the first book since Michener's *Hawaii*, I really could not put down. Phyllis has done an amazing amount of research. . . . I hope we may see many more books come from this fertile mind.

—Ruth Naylor

Fascinating book. Gunderson has really done her research.

—Art Stacey

Phyllis Gunderson delivers a masterfully written story, with great wit and insight. *The Jaguar Prophecies* fringes on the imaginable. You will find yourself considering the possibilities and turning page after page.

—Bob Waddell

The Jaguar Prophecies is funny, mysterious, and can lead you to further investigations as it did me. I was intrigued enough to read more about ancient civilizations, their customs, mythology, and art.

—Estel Murdock

Phyllis Gunderson has taken historical and scientific material and woven it masterfully into a novel that is clever, captivating, and provocative. Her heroine, Matt Howard, has the knowledge and personality to keep the reader enthralled from beginning to end. The ancients have passed on to us what they knew would be coming in our day. We had better listen to the prophecies symbolized by the jaguar.

—Kisi Watkins

The new term "faction" describes Phyllis Gunderson's book perfectly. While the book is fiction, her research and attention to detail are solid.

—Wendy DeWitt

I couldn't put it down—my children didn't get a meal for two days. On a topic that could be doomsday and depressing, this book gives hope with humor.

—Kiana Berrey

THE
JAGUAR
PROPHECIES

PHYLLIS GUNDERSON

CFI
Springville, Utah

This is a work of fiction. The characters, names, incidents, places, and dialogue are products of the author's imagination, and are not to be construed as real.

ISBN 13: 978-1-59955-462-4

Published by CFI, an imprint of Cedar Fort, Inc., 2373 W. 700 S., Springville, UT 84663
Distributed by Cedar Fort, Inc., www.cedarfort.com

LIBRARY OF CONGRESS CATALOGING-IN-PUBLICATION DATA

Gunderson, Phyllis.
  The jaguar prophecies / Phyllis Gunderson.
    p. cm.
  ISBN 978-1-59955-462-4
  1. Women archaeologists--Fiction. 2. Jaguar--Fiction. 3. Maya
calendar--Fiction. 4. Mexico--Fiction. I. Title.

  PS3607.U5475J34 2010
  813'.6--dc22

        2010026354

Cover design by Angela D. Olsen
Cover design © 2010 by Lyle Mortimer
Edited and typeset by Heidi Doxey

Printed in the United States of America

10 9 8 7 6 5 4 3 2 1

Printed on acid-free paper

CONTENTS

CONTENTS

ONE

09.21.2004 / YUCATAN PENINSULA / CHICHEN ITZA

"*Señora?* Madam?" A young man's worried voice came from slightly below the raised, covered platform I sat on. "I am sorry to telling you, please to forgive me, but you have the wrong place."

I looked down into the black eyes of a teenage boy, the smooth brown skin above his top lip punctured by a sparse mustache. Behind him, my view took in the north side of the Pyramid of Kukulcan, its ninety-one step stairway anchored by two massive serpent heads on the ground. The pyramid plaza already teemed with tourists jostling for the best view before the celestial show began. In an hour the sun would shine on the balustrade of the stairs, projecting a diamond-patterned rattlesnake that would gradually slither to the stone serpent head before it disappeared into the earth. I had no intention of leaving my comfortable, shaded chair. Middle age has its rewards.

"Is this the area," I asked the boy on the ground, "where the equinox sunlight looks like a snake crawling down the steps of the pyramid?"

"Yes, ma'am, but—"

"And this," I pointed to a heavy plastic sign, "says these eight chairs are reserved for the Barbachano family and their guest?"

1

"Yes, ma'am."

"Then I'm in the right place." I smiled serenely without showing teeth. "I'm their guest."

He squirmed and then announced, "My name is Leonardo Barbachano, and our guest is Dr. M. Howard."

"I'm Dr. Matt Howard." I'd been saddled with "Mathilda" at birth, due to the temporary hormonal imbalance of my mother. I legally changed the name to Matt as soon as I could sign the paperwork.

The boy stared a moment and then blurted, "You are a lady."

"Well, thank you, Leonardo. At my age, very few people notice."

Leonardo, nonplussed and embarrassed, pleaded, "*Lo siento.* Sorry, you will come with me?"

The boy could have wrestled me out of my place if he wanted to, so I hunkered deeper into the chair, theoretically making myself heavier. Pawing through my pack, I found the invitation forwarded to me from the anthropology department at my university in Arizona. I teach archaeology, but anthropology is next of kin. There must have been a mix-up in the departments.

Dear Dr. Howard,

The Barbachano family is pleased to send this invitation for the fall equinox sun phenomenon at the Pyramid of Kukulcan. Enclosed is a ticket for entrance into Chichen Itza, plus airfare to Merida and a rental car. There will be a shaded platform where you can view the event which begins at 4:00 PM. Accommodations that evening will be provided. We are anxious to discuss your article.

Thank you.

Yup, it was the right paper. I wondered which of my archaeology articles had caught their interest. "Mr. Barbachano," I said, thinking formality would make the kid feel important. "I'm an archaeologist, Dr. Matt Howard, and here is the invitation from your family." I handed the paper to him and explained, "I have, of course, been to Chichen Itza professionally, but I've never seen the sun-snake move down the stairs."

Nothing is worth seeing if you have to fight 50,000 tourists. The influx of gawkers at the spring and fall equinoxes began in the 1980s, increasing every year by several thousand.

"Dr. Howard," the boy said, "please to forgive me again, you have the, how do you say, iten . . . identi . . ." His eyebrows knotted over the difficult word. I inched toward compassion—my first mistake.

"The word is 'identification,'" I explained. "If you say 'ID,' everyone will understand." I was kind, thoughtful, reverent, cheerful, brave, and stupid as I pulled out my driver's license. The hateful photo looked older than my actual age of . . . okay, late forties. It galled me to know I was stuck with the picture until I had to get a new license, at which time I would be as old as the picture looked.

I let the boy take my license as if it were a visual aid—my second grave error. He skimmed it, scanned me, and then folded the license inside my invitation and pushed both into the back pocket of his drooping jeans. "You are a different Dr. Howard," he said. "Please follow me." He turned and walked away. I had just broken the first survival rule of travelers: never give your ID to anyone.

Grabbing my backpack, I launched myself down the three steps separating the platform from the ground. When I caught up to the boy, I used the voice that intimidates my students. "Give back my papers, or I'll call the authorities and have you arrested."

He answered calmly, definitely not worried. "I will return your identification papers when the Old One has seen you." He pronounced "identification" just dandy. The little rat had tricked me, playing on my motherly instincts—not that I have any to spare. Everything nature gave me is currently directed toward my adopted Chinese daughter, Marisa, because she's at the ugly age of thirteen where she pretends she doesn't know who I am and orders me not to come to her seventh-grade classes for any reason. My experience with Marisa gave me confidence in reading teenagers, but this young man pulled a fast one, and I dropped like an anvil. Maybe I could round up some sympathy by playing my little-old-lady card.

"I hope we'll be back in time to see the show," I said, allowing a plaintive catch to form in my throat as I scurried to keep up. "The invitation gave instructions to find the platform, but I'm glad to stand on the plaza with," I paused only slightly, "the other tourists. Please return my *i-dent-i-fi-ca-tion*." I enunciated the word slowly, with an edge of sarcasm, so he'd know I'd caught his ruse. The boy smiled, proud to have outwitted me. He pulled a cell phone from one of his voluminous pant's pockets, dialed quickly, and spewed a stream of Spanish to someone on the line. Then he nodded, closed the phone, and made his way through the thickening crowd. I had no choice but to follow.

We weaved like dancers through the dense bodies, our arms lifting and lowering to avoid contact as we breathed in the wet smells of mashed people. I brushed against their drops of sweat to pool with my own, consoling myself that the situation might have been worse: I could have given the kid my passport.

Leonardo led me to the base of Kukulcan, the west edge of the north staircase, where he stooped to unlock a small door that was hidden in the shadows of the giant balustrade. Craning my neck above the crowd, I caught a vision of the shaded platform, my place of honor still empty, and I briefly considered fighting my way back and letting the boy keep my driver's license. A fat lot of good it would do him with my picture on it. But I'm an archaeologist, and I knew what lay behind his door. An older pyramid had been discovered inside Kukulcan in the 1930s. The blood in my veins, the very marrow of my bones, wouldn't let me walk away. The tall boy, bending at the waist, held the door open and motioned for me to enter the black hole.

I'm a slow learner. I obeyed.

"Young man," I said as he closed the door, leaving us in darkness, "what gives you the authority to open that door?"

A blast of steady light illuminated his grinning face as he held an electric lantern above us. "The Mexican government controls the buildings," he said. "But my family owns the land. We have . . . privileges." He nodded at my backpack. "You should to leave your bag here."

"After what you just did to me?" I guffawed a large "ha" at him. "There's not a chance I'll leave my bag for you to steal."

He shrugged. "I cannot to help you up the stairs. My one hand holds the light, my number two hand must climb."

"I'll take the risk," I shot back, clutching the bag to my chest.

My young guide turned, and we moved single file, bent double, through the tight little tunnel. My pack swung from my arm, hitting my leg every second step. The stones seemed splotched with green color, and I twisted my head to see details, which was why I tripped on the first stair of the inner pyramid as we moved sharply right and upward. Using the term "stair" would be an undeserved compliment. It was more of a stone ladder and had to be negotiated in an upright crawling position. The light ahead bobbed as Leonardo ascended with one hand, the other holding the light higher for my benefit. He seemed like a nice kid, but I'd been wrong before. The study of people is not my best subject, which is the reason I like archaeology. Dead things are manageable, unlike a boy with a lantern.

There wasn't room to wear the pack on my back, so I hefted it up and forward with grunts and occasional moans. The heat turned vicious in the cramped environment. I stopped counting steps and concentrated on the required crawl. If I stood upright, I'd hit my head before doing a free fall down the lumps masquerading as stairs. The youth above me moved fast, even though his knee-to-chest posture was certainly more uncomfortable than my hunchback position. Surrounded by massive stones, the feeling of being buried alive in a crypt caused my resolve to crumble.

"Mr. Barbachano," I called up. There was a slight flat echo, and the light stopped moving. "I don't think I can climb anymore." It was a stupid statement, since I'd already reached the point of no return. Going down the stairs would be as treacherous as continuing the upward climb.

The boy's voice rolled down the stairs toward me. "The top is almost here." I figured he was lying to keep me crawling. When the light suddenly stopped and got brighter, I knew Leonardo had reached the summit. Throwing my pack up two stairs at a time, I grunted my way to it and repeated the action with resolve. Puffing past the last crumbling step, I collapsed on a flat surface, my cheek against a stone floor that felt strangely cool. Leonardo allowed me some time to rest and then waited while I struggled to a standing position.

We were in a chamber with the statue of Chac Mool in the center. I had always wondered about the impossible position of the reclining Aztec sacrificial god: lying on his rounded back, knees bent, head lifted to stare at some mysterious thing at his right. Chac Mool's flat stomach held the plate meant for hearts ripped from living victims. The god looked so uncomfortable, it was no wonder he was grouchy enough to devour beating hearts.

"Dr. Howard," Leo quietly interrupted my thoughts. "Come." He gestured to the opening of another room, flanked by pillars. As Leo raised his lantern, the light focused on a red bench carved of stone. The armrest was shaped into a fierce jaguar head facing us, frozen in a snarl, with insets of pyrite eyes and fangs. As the light rose higher, I saw the flat white eyes of a skeletal old man sitting on the jaguar throne. The sight tightened my gut, and my bag dropped to the dust. Focusing on the unglazed, dead eyes, I thought the figure was a dried-out mummy until a movement of breath lifted its naked chest. His skin folded over itself in ancient wrinkles, the muscles of his arms resembled chicken tendons, his nose was classic Mayan like the top half of a beak. A guard stood on the left side of the blind man, and the mottled stone behind them looked like wallpaper.

"It is the Old One," Leo whispered as we moved forward.

The guard spoke to the boy in speedy Spanish. Unfortunately,

I'd learned the language in slow motion. Nobody speaks it that way. Leo shot back rapid-fire words, his head tilting in my direction. The guard bent to speak in the old man's ear, not Spanish but Nahuatl or Maya Quiche, or it could have been Sanskrit for all I knew. The ancient relic sat silent and then uttered a few guttural sounds to the guard who relayed the message to Leonardo.

Leo turned to me. "The Old One says you are a woman."

So much for profound wisdom. I'd been taken hostage by a teenage thief, a mostly dead shaman, and a hefty henchman. My need to get away put a spot of unaccustomed fear in my stomach. "Look, folks," I tried to sound bold, "I got your invitation, it sounded fun, but now the fun's over." I turned to Leonardo. "If you'll return my papers, I'll be running along." Leo and the guard exchanged a look I couldn't read by lantern light. "Leonardo Barbachano," I spoke his full name, full force, implying the threat of possible danger, "give me my driver's license."

Leo's eyes widened, the guard retreated a pace, and the spooky, white-eyed Mayan turned his lifeless orbs on me. I stared back with the definite feeling that the Old One could see me even without eyes. My scalp shifted, making a soft sound inside my head like taffeta, and the fear vanished. The Old One uttered a single scratched word, his guard spoke five, and Leo said, "The Old One invites you to stay for the ceremony and sleep tonight at the Hacienda."

"He said all that in one word?" I was incredulous.

Leonardo whispered. "I do not know his word. I do not understand the ancient tongue."

Now I was curious. "Ask what the word means."

After a short exchange with the guard, Leo replied, "The word is 'mark' in the old language."

"Mark what?" I didn't like the sound of it.

He hesitated. "Mark you."

I envisioned some kind of tattoo. "I don't think I'll take you up on the 'mark' thing," I replied. "I'll just watch the ceremony and stay at the Hacienda, thank you. But before we leave, I have a few questions for the Old One, if that's all right." I'm inquisitive to the core.

Leo began the translation process, but the ancient, twisted twig of a man interrupted with croaked words to the guard, who relayed the message.

My teenage guide turned to me. "He gives permission to ask questions." The blind Mayan could either understand English or read minds. Either option made me nervous. I faced him squarely, filled with the courage of a cockroach.

"Why did your people build new pyramids over old ones?" Current thinking favored competition and pride among rulers, as in, "My pyramid is bigger than your pyramid." The old priest's answer might add flavor to the controversy.

Leo translated for me. "The stars command where a pyramid stands. It becomes sacred ground. Many years pass, the stars change, the pyramid cannot give correct time. A new pyramid is built on top and," Leo used his hands to show rotation, "changed to again show signs in the sky to keep the cycles."

"They built massive stone buildings to tell the time?" I'd be laughed off the stage if I shared that with my colleagues. Primitive people didn't have that kind of science.

Gibberish in Nahuatl/Quiche and Spanish eventually reached my ears in English. When the answers organized themselves in my mind, the hugeness of it went past possibility. These people tracked cosmic time over thousands of years, in cycles designed to forecast galactic events. They predicted equinoxes, solstices, sunspot and solar eclipse cycles hundreds of years before their occurrence. Priests recorded changes in the sky for untold generations.

"How did your people learn this . . . skill?" I was going to add "impossible" but sanity prevailed.

Leonardo did the obscure translation. "From the people who came before."

Frustrated, I spoke directly to the blind man responsible for this nonsense. "Who *are* you?"

The three men did their translation mumbo-jumbo, and Leo answered. "He is the last priest before the end time. He is the final keeper of cycle five. He carries the warning."

A low frustrated growl escaped my throat. "What's the end time, the fifth cycle, and the warning?" I thought I saw the hint of a smile add creases to the old man's mouth but attributed it to bad lighting. A new wrinkle wouldn't put a dent in that ancient, furrowed face. Leo babbled, the guard spoke mush, and the Old One ground out his reply. Then the process reversed, and Leo spoke to me.

"The end time of the fifth age is when the sun rises in *Xibalba be.*"

I looked at the boy, cocked my head, and raised my eyebrows in a universal query. *"Xibalba be?"*

"It is the name of the center place in the sky that Earth will face soon. We have not been there for . . ." Leo concentrated on the words, ". . . for twenty-six thousand years. We live now in the number five cycle, which is five thousand years and . . . uh . . . a little more."

The kid had beads of sweat on his forehead and needed a compliment. "You're a good translator, Leonardo."

He studied his feet and shook his head. "Numbers are hard."

"And the warning?"

"The world must get ready for *Nawal Tijax.*"

Patience, Matt, patience. "And what does 'Nawal Tee-hash' mean?"

"I do not speak the old language."

What a crock of cryptic nonsense. My voice rose a few decibels. "Leo, please. I want answers, not riddles. And then I want my driver's license."

Eventually more verbiage exchanged between Leo, the guard, the decrepit mummy, and me brought understanding. Apparently Mayans believe the ages of the past have been divided into five cycles, each lasting a little more than five thousand years, that always end in massive destructions. Then the survivors start over. This time, however, a double whammy swings above humanity's collective head. Along with ordinary annihilation, the earth enters *Xibalba be* to face the center of the galaxy, an event which happens every twenty-six thousand years.

I felt sorry for the rickety priest who sat on the jaguar throne with the burden to warn the world. Nobody would pay the slightest attention to his convoluted legend. It was a complicated little myth, not useful as a bedtime story, and certainly not worth building pyramids over existing pyramids. Curiosity, however, held me in place like a suction cup.

"So, what's going to happen?" I asked. "And how can people get ready?" The three men exchanged speeches, reviewed them again, and finally Leo turned to me.

"He doesn't know."

In my astonishment I used poor judgment, my default setting, when I turned to the old man and said, "Your warning is worthless if you can't tell what to expect and how to prepare."

There was silence in the tomb. My ears got hot as the old Mayan's sightless eyes bore into my brain. After waiting an interminable amount of time, his response wove its way through the three tongues.

"Your people burned our books."

"My people didn't . . ." I stopped, remembering that the Spanish threw Mayan codices into bonfires when they conquered Mexico. The event represented an irretrievable, tragic loss to history. Apparently, the books contained vital information about the end of the fifth cycle plus the *Xibalba be* event. The last chapter of the story had disappeared. I softened toward the creased, white-eyed figure on the throne and quietly said, "I'm sorry."

His answer flew at me with the speed of light. When Leo translated, there was still a trace of anger in the command. "*You must complete the jaguar prophecies.*"

I ignored the cryptic command and protested to the three men, not waiting for translations. "My people were Danish—they didn't burn your books. I'm just an ordinary archaeologist, and your loss is not my fault. I apologize for taking someone else's place who might have helped you. Maybe you can find *him*." I put emphasis on "him" before I finished the speech. "My invitation was just a simple mistake." I bowed awkwardly and turned to leave the inner room, bumping into Chac Mool, who still stared into the darkness of the pyramid staircase. Searching the floor for my backpack, I suddenly froze when words traveled through the air to crawl into my ears, a hoarse frog sound, like the death rattle of a dying man heard from a long distance away.

"There . . . are . . . no . . . mistakes."

I whirled around to find Leonardo next to me. "Did you . . . ?" I stammered. "Did he . . . ?" I peered into the gloom of the throne room, grabbed Leo's arm to lift his lantern higher, and saw only the white fangs of the jaguar throne, empty of its occupant from moments before.

"Where did he go?"

"Who?"

"Don't play games with me, Mr. Barbachano. You know who—the Old One and his henchman." I strode back to the small throne room and pushed against the walls for a hidden passage. Leo set his lantern on the floor, the light shadowing his face into a Halloween ghoul. I cringed at the sight.

"Dr. Howard," Leo said, "we must go. They wait." He scooped up his lantern. "I will go first. If you fall I am able to stop you."

"If I land on top of you, little buddy," I said grimly, "you'll flatten like a snowboard, and we'll speed to the bottom like an Alpine slide. How did the Old One disappear?"

Leo sounded weary, his voice lifting from the edge of the staircase. "We go this way." He and his light descended into the abyss. Suddenly aware of the harsh heat and cruel blackness, I had to follow the boy again. But I did it grudgingly, convinced there was a secret passage somewhere.

I descended backwards, dragging my pack like a counter-weight above me. My breathing soon became shallow and difficult, as if we'd used most of the available air.

"Why did it get hot all of a sudden?" I puffed the words down at him. "It wasn't this bad in the room."

"It is hot here always. You did not feel it when you saw the Old One."

"Is he a hypnotist?"

"I do not know."

"How old is he?"

"I do not know."

The boy struggled to hold the light for both of us as we dropped, slipped, and slithered down the dilapidated staircase. When we reached the floor, I stretched out face down across the bottom steps, my aching body in a posture of gratitude.

Leo had no mercy. "Dr. Howard, they wait."

"Who's waiting?" The words muffled themselves into the stone.

"The people of the ceremony."

Hungry, thirsty, dirty, and tired, I no longer cared about witnessing their little ritual. I pushed myself against the ancient stairs to an upright position, groaning out the words, "I hope there's a banquet out there."

Leo switched the lantern off and opened the door. A rush of cool air hit my back and, with some exertion, I met the night, which was lit by the moon's lantern, accompanied by stars.

"I guess I missed the snake show," I said sarcastically as we exited the inner vault.

"The snake comes for tourists two times a year," Leo whispered. "Now, you will see what tourists do not see."

A crowd of at least a hundred stood, silent and unmoving, at the base of the north stairs. A woman standing at the edge of the assembly placed a half coconut of liquid in my hands. I nodded and smiled weakly, eagerly drinking the sweet contents. I figured I could medicate for parasites later. The group parted into a semi-circle as Leo led me to the center, facing Kukulcan.

"I just want to observe," I whispered. "Put me in the back."

His reply was a hissed command. "Do nothing. Say nothing." He abandoned me and melted into the crowd.

I looked up at the background of stars, which seemed like brilliant spotlights on a stage. Someone began with a single clap of hands. Immediately, a bird chirped twice. Another clap, two more chirps. Searching the pyramid, I expected to see a person, a tape recorder, even a bird, but the moon illuminated only empty steps. Others joined in synchronized clapping, and the bird added its chorus. I tried to formulate explanations for the bird sounds, theorizing that the height and depth of the stairs produced an echo. Clapping rhythms bounced off the lower steps, producing a high-pitched squeal. Almost simultaneously, sound bounced from the higher section, longer and lower. The pyramid produced not a mimic of clapping but the caw of a quetzal bird, ingeniously engineered into the tall, shallow steps.

Those were my last lucid thoughts.

The gathered humans whispered a word, and a rhythm surfaced: "quetzal *clap* quetzal." I recognized the name of the quetzal bird, representative of the god Quetzalcoatl or Kukulcan. Shaking my head to clear it resulted in an uncontrolled wobble, and I suspected that my coconut drink had more than coconuts in it. The atmosphere discharged an electric hum, and my effort to cling to reality dissolved as the clapping merged with the reverberating rhythm of feet on the ground. My own feet melted into the earth, and I no longer felt them as I leaned from side to side in rhythm with the natives chanting the name of their god.

The invisible bird emitted a piercing shriek, reverberating into the air. A crashing cacophony of echoes ricocheted off the ancient edifice into the star-filled heavens. I turned faint with the sounds, the rhythm, the drumming feet on the earth, and the swaying people. Placing my hands on my ears, I tried to block the noise from my head with fingers that felt strangely numb. Yet it penetrated my skin, submerging me in . . .

Silence.

TWO

I woke with a headache the size of Colorado. Opening one eye, the light burned a halo through it, forcing me to shut it again. There was a soft bed beneath me. It felt clean, though I still wore my grimy, sweaty clothes from yesterday, minus shoes. I sighed in relief. If I thought some stranger had put me in pajamas, my arms limp, mouth drooling, I would keep my eyes shut against the humiliation until they loaded me into the rental car to catch my plane. Slowly opening one eye again, I viewed a cheery room with white curtains at the window and colorful Mexican pottery displayed on dark wood tables. Then I opened the other eye to analyze a ceiling fan whirring pleasantly above my head. I was probably at the Barbachano Hacienda. Pounding pain in my frontal lobe forced both eyes shut again as I rolled to my side, grunting.

A mature female voice drifted from a probable doorway. "You are awake, Dr. Howard?" Her English carried a heavy accent, but it sounded sultry, admirable. "Hi," I said, eyes still closed. "Sorry I can't greet you in person, but everything hurts."

"Claro," she said. "You . . . how do you say . . . fall down?"

"I fainted?" I said aloud to the dark behind my eyes. "In front of witnesses?" They must have rolled my floppy body onto a stretcher and carried me to the hotel. Egads, I'd never fainted in my life. "I'm embarrassed," I told the unseen woman.

"Please to be not. The . . . eh . . . time of quetzal es difícil for the marked one."

My eyes opened wide. "I got marked?"

I saw a lovely older woman with a glass on a tray. Her dark hair, dusted in grey, was gathered in a bun at the nape of her neck. She wore a white peasant blouse and embroidered skirt in bright colors that hurt my eyes.

"Sí, madam," she said. "El viejo give you great honor."

I groaned. "I need to get rid of this headache before I ask questions."

"I have la medicina here." She set the tray on the table by the bed. "I leave you por veinte minutos." *Twenty minutes.*

I had the presence of mind to thank her through the throbbing. There were no pills, only a glass filled with liquid that smelled like coconuts mixed with rotting fish. I drank the vile stuff and lay back on the pillow, waiting to conquer the agony and wondering if they'd poisoned me. I'd been marked, probably with an indelible tattoo on my forehead that would require stupid bangs to cover it. I'd once seen a movie where a woman in the jungle had been decorated with permanent juice while she was asleep. She wore it the rest of her life. Rats. I was marked. I spent the twenty minutes wallowing in self-pity, reviewing how I'd been tricked into a trap.

When the woman returned, she brought towels. My head had cleared, and I tottered to a mirror above the dresser to stare at my bleary, blotched face. A tattoo might have improved it, but there wasn't one. My relief exuded itself in a giggle.

"I thought you said I was marked."

"Jes. At the night of yesterday."

"Where's the mark?"

"It cannot to be . . . to see." She laughed. "My English, it is—"

"Your English is beautiful," I finished for her, euphoric that there was no visible mark on my face beyond the ones I had earned: a hairline scar across my nose when I fell off the swings trying to go all the way around; the blemish on my chin from combining Coke and Mentos candy, which exploded in my face; the burn on my forehead produced by a hot curling iron I didn't know how to use. No tattoos or staining juice. I turned from the mirror, smiling.

The lady offered her hand. "My name is Maria Barbachano. You will be please to dress. We have to do much." After showering and changing into clean clothes, I re-entered the room where the angel of mercy waited.

"Hello," I said to her, pain free and presentable. "I'm Matt Howard. Thank you for your kindness."

She smiled. "Welcome to La Hacienda Chichen. Please to follow me."

We left my room, which opened onto an outdoor patio filled with potted plants and a profusion of flowers. To my left was a large pool and terrace. Hacienda Chichen was a resort, and a splendid one at that. We walked ahead to the main house. My cheap watch said it was 10:30. My stomach growled its hunger at me.

"Is there a restaurant anywhere near?"

"Jes, pero . . . you cannot to eat. Follow, please. He will explain."

I'd done a lot of following since yesterday. No point quitting now. She led me into the main building and then down a hall to a small room. It was filled with an oval table where three men sat, wearing navy suits and ties. All had black hair, dark eyes, and small mustaches. An air conditioner hummed its melody from a window, which explained how they could be wearing suits and ties. Maria softly closed the door as she left the room.

"Thank you for joining us. Please be seated." The man's speech was smooth and natural, without an accent. A hand-painted rose decorated his tie. I sat. He slid some papers toward me. "Did you write this?" It was an article titled "Precession and the Maya" by M. Howard. "That's my name," I said, "but I didn't write it." The three men quietly grunted at each other, a kind of

'I-told-you" acknowledgement. So, they all understood English, but Mr. Flower-tie held the floor.

"How did you get the invitation?" *Well, that was abrupt. Does he think I stole it?*

I turned defensive. "Who were you trying to send it to?"

"I addressed it to the man from the astronomy department who wrote this article." He pointed to the short bio that accompanied the article. Dr. M. Howard was apparently a professor of astronomy at my university.

"Well, it ended up at the anthropology department, and they sent it on to me, since my name was on the envelope. I checked the tickets and it all looked legitimate, but you didn't leave a name or number so I could ask which of my articles you had an interest in." I smiled at my own gullibility, thinking I had written something so profound I'd get tickets to Chichen Itza. "I'm an archaeologist and write several articles a year," . . . *okay, two* . . . "so you can see how the mistake happened. When I get home, I'll look up Professor Howard and tell him I accidentally took his vacation. Maybe you can start over." I came to within half a second of offering to pay back the tickets and airfare before I remembered I hadn't even seen the sun's equinox snake show. They could pay for their own incompetence.

Mr. Flower-tie spoke. "The Old One says you are the one."

I sat straighter, an effort at authority. "I'm not the one. I teach graduate-level archaeology and one undergrad Sumerian literature class. Other than recognizing Orion and the Big Dipper, I know very little about astronomy. Face it, guys, you've made a mistake."

The Three Amigos glanced at each other before the main speaker said, "The Old One believes there are no—"

"—mistakes," I cut in. "He's wrong. Whatever you want me to do, I can't do it."

He leaned toward me. "You must warn your people."

"Not the whole world?"

He didn't catch my sarcasm. "Only your people."

"What will happen to 'my people' if I don't tip them off?"

"They will die." He spoke the words in a matter-of-fact way that increased the impact of their meaning. "They might die anyway, but they must have a chance to survive. That is our purpose and one we faithfully carried for five thousand one hundred twenty-five years, since the last age."

I surrendered. "Okay, I'll play your game for a while. What disasters happened in the last four ages?"

"We know only the memory of legends. The Popol Vuh has stories, but they tell of humans turning into monkeys, fish, and birds to survive." He raised one dark, hairy eyebrow. "Your people don't accept myth and legend. I won't bore you." I kept silent but tipped my head quizzically to the side. Maybe he thought I'd lose interest, but I waited. He finally shrugged. "The first cycle ended in famine, maybe a climate change, we don't know. Humans were hunted and eaten by animals."

"Turnabout is fair," I said. "And the second age?"

"Ended by a strong wind."

"No details?"

"A *very* strong wind."

"Good enough. And cycle number three?"

"Destroyed in a rain of fiery, poisonous ashes."

"Sounds like volcanoes."

He nodded. "The fourth age was water."

"Any connection to Genesis?"

"The legend speaks of a married couple who escaped in a boat with animals."

"That's Genesis," I said, resting my chin on my hand. "What's the prognosis for our fifth age?"

"Our time is called *Nahui-Olin*, the Age of Earthquake."

I considered his statement for a moment and then dropped my hand to the table, leaning back. "And then what happens?"

"The cycle begins again."

I tried to be polite but couldn't quite pull it off. "If everything begins again, why the big push to send out warnings no one will believe?"

The man bowed his head, took in a deep breath, and exhaled

loudly, as if my skull was too thick to crack. Then he said, "Because, this time we also face *Xibalba be*, the Mayan name for the dark rift in the center of the universe. We have no records of what it will do. We are told that, without preparation, there might be no life left on Earth."

"Haven't we survived it before? We're still here."

He spoke to me as if I had a hearing handicap. "Our calendars only cover a single Great Round. We have no records of entering the dark rift twenty-six thousand years ago. Maybe man survived, but maybe life had to be seeded here again." He shrugged.

"Look," I began, while internally coaching myself: *Be nice, Matt. Respect his traditions.* "Shouldn't you inform governments?"

He gave a short, mirthless laugh. "They already know and will save themselves."

I stared at him, confused and disbelieving. "I don't like what you're telling me."

His tone was a challenge. "How would you rescue six billion people?"

"I'd at least give them a chance to get ready."

The flower-tie gentleman shook his head. "Official announcements would cause panic. Law would be useless. Governments would collapse."

"So," I took a deep breath of cool air produced by the humming machine. "Governments know there's danger ahead, but they're keeping the annihilation of the world as a planned surprise."

"You and others will carry the message."

"You want me to tell people that the end of our little five-thousand-year age will be caused by earthquakes, but the real danger comes from a place in the universe called *Xibalba be*. I'll get locked in a loony bin. Don't you have a clue of what's coming?"

"We believe the marked ones will be led to knowledge."

"Well, Mr. . . . I don't even know your name."

"Barbachano," he proudly said. "Our family owned Chichen Itza for many generations. The government took the buildings from us for their tourist industry, but we still own the land. We are descended from ancient priests who tracked the stars. We keep the sacred trust."

"Well, Mr. Barbachano, it's been nice meeting you. I'll consider your suggestion to warn people and get back to you if I decide to join your project." I stood to leave, intending never to see this family again.

"Dr. Howard," he said. "You are marked."

My reply was hot enough to singe his eyebrows. "I checked. There's no mark. I'm going home." I walked to the door and opened it.

"By the way," he said, before I could shut the door, "don't eat anything for forty-eight hours."

"Why? "

"You can drink pure water," he advised, "but you will deeply regret eating."

"I deeply regret coming here."

Mr. Barbachano produced a smile almost tinged with kindness. "Do you have any more questions before you leave to catch your plane?"

"Yes." I remembered the untranslated words of the Old One. "What does Nawal Tee-hash mean?"

The man's smile faded into grimness. "Nawal Tijax is from the old tongue. It is the double bladed knife. Day of Suffering is its name, the end of the Great Cycle."

I leaned against the door frame. "Do you have any good news?"

"You can save many people." He spread his arms with open hands, a gesture meaning "what more do you want?"

I groaned and closed the door. On my way out of the lobby, I passed the restaurant, which wafted smells of spices and chicken, pork and tamales. I reacted instinctively and soon found myself sitting at a table with no memory of how I got there. The waitress handed me a menu, and my tongue swam through saliva. But when my words came out, I ordered only two bottles of water. These people had turned me into a superstitious old fool.

In my room I packed and then walked to the street. A car waited out front, and Leonardo waved from behind the wheel.

"I will take you to your car," he said. The resort bordered the ruins, and the drive was short. Fortunately, the rental hadn't been vandalized.

He smiled and handed me a small envelope. "Here is your i-den-ti-fi-ca-tion."

Shaking my head over his stratagem from yesterday, I took the papers and exited his car.

"Dr. Howard?" The boy was solemn. "My father said to give you this." It was the article on precession, written by the astronomer with my name.

I grunted, grabbed the magazine, and, unlocking the rental, slid behind the wheel. "Tell your dad I've made no commitment." When I turned the key, Leo moved to the car window and leaned in.

"Dr. Howard?"

"What is it now?"

"Be careful not to eat until tomorrow night."

My eyes shot a voltage of anger into the boy. "Is anyone going to tell me why?"

The kid grinned at me, face lit up with perverse delight. "If you do, you will wish you had, instead, the headache."

"And why would that be?"

"The mark needs time to . . . what is the word? . . . develop. Food makes it slow. Please believe us."

"You and your family can take your mark and—" He eagerly waited for me to teach him new words that I'd regret later. Instead, I shoved the car into gear and drove off into the hot horizon.

THREE

An uneventful flight is soon forgotten. Unless you're hungry. In that case, every minute sears itself into your memory banks. I drank water like a camel, which meant I was continually standing in line for the tiny cubicle they call a restroom—more like being crammed into a high school locker with the door slammed shut. By the time I landed in Phoenix and picked up Marisa at her friend's house, I was not my usual jovial self. Marisa hadn't been herself since she entered puberty and junior high, at least six months ago. She huffed into the car and slammed the door. I maintained an even tone as I maneuvered the car onto the freeway.

"Did you enjoy staying with your new friend?"

She made me wait in silence before she growled, "No."

"Do you wish you'd stayed with the Allens, like the good old days?"

She turned on me, her upper lip curled. "I'm old enough to be alone."

I made the mistake of a quick laugh. "You're thirteen. I'd go to jail for child neglect."

Marisa turned her face to the side window, snarling. "That would be a tragedy."

"What did you say?"

"Nothing."

I attempted tough love. "Young lady," I said with authority, "you are on the verge of being grounded for the rest of junior high."

She still spoke to her side window. "Big deal. I'm already your prisoner."

I glanced toward her but saw only the back of her long, dark hair. This wasn't standard adolescent behavior. I'd bought and read the parenting books, scavenged indexes for "rude, surly, hateful, and irritable," and suspected the experts didn't have children of their own. Dr. Spock didn't, and look what he did to us.

I attempted soft love. "Marisa, tell me what's wrong. I love you dearly. I'm your mother."

Her words came at me like projectiles from a nail gun. "You are *not* my mother. My real mother is in China, searching for me. But she'll never find me because you took me away."

It was hardly a secret that Marisa had been adopted. She's a slender Chinese girl with delicate features. I'm a sturdy Scandinavian with splotched skin. Until now, it hadn't been an issue. I tried smooth love. "I don't know what happened to your birth mom, sweetheart. No one could tell me, but you'd been in the orphanage your whole life until the day I came to get you. We've talked about this many times."

"If you hadn't stolen me,"—emphasis on the word *stolen*—"she would have come back for me. You ruined my life."

So far, tough love, soft love, and smooth love hadn't worked. We drove home in silence. Marisa bolted from the car while it was still rolling to a stop in our garage. By the time I got inside she had disappeared, which was fine with me. I unpacked in peace, colored with anger.

I didn't make dinner since I wasn't eating, and if Marisa was so set on being independent, I figured she could fend for herself. When she emerged from her cave and saw nothing prepared, she glared at me.

I leaned on the table, the inside of my arms stretched tight.

"Let's talk, and I'll fix dinner for you."

Marisa stared at my left arm and said in disgust, "You're dirty." She turned on her heels and left the room, satisfied with her insult. I looked down to see brown lines on the inside of my elbow, forming the beginnings of a three-inch design. I yelped and rushed to the sink where I ran hot water over it, putting enough soap on the area to wash a load of clothes. I used rubbing alcohol, scouring powder, and petroleum jelly until the skin was close to bleeding, but nothing touched the mark. It wasn't a tattoo, more like a fine-point permanent marker. Those wretched people had put their stain on the inside of my elbow. Moving to my own bathroom, I dabbed make-up on the mark. It was like trying to hide a black scar with watercolors. I decided to make an appointment with a dermatologist to remove the ugly thing. If the Barbachano family thought adding a mark would convince me to join their team, they were . . . well . . . really wrong.

In the middle of the night, I heard Marisa rummaging in the kitchen, banging pots and lids and noisily opening cans. I smiled smugly, satisfied to know my little nemesis was hungry too. The next morning Marisa and I brushed egos in our hurry to get to our respective schools—her junior high and my university. I briefly wondered if I could sue the Chinese government for selling me a defective model without instructions. But she'd been the source of utter joy in my life until now. Maybe Chinese DNA exploded during hormonal growth and repaired itself during adulthood. All the Asian folks I knew were superb specimens of humanity. In any case, I couldn't trade Marisa in for a perfect seven-year-old.

The journey to campus took me from my air-conditioned car to an air-conditioned classroom, requiring only four breaths of hot air in between. It was the heat from Marisa that created blisters. My Sumerian class was a welcome distraction. We were preparing oral reports on the contributions of the Sumerians to civilization. I described possible topics in glowing terms.

"So, to review," I said at the end of class, pointing to Sumerian accomplishments on the board, "the discovery of the library at

Nineveh uncovered a previously unknown civilization that had flourished long before Babylon and Egypt. They invented writing, irrigation canals, the making of bronze, the potter's wheel and kiln, medicine, agriculture, and schools. Their mathematical system was sexagesimal—" Guffaws erupted on cue. In the many years I'd given this lecture, a few bumpkins always sniggered over the word *sex* in any context. I ignored the distraction.

"To explain," I persisted, "the Sumerians used a base of 60, which we still use in our hours, minutes, and in the 360 degree circle. They were able to divide fractions, multiply into the millions, and calculate roots, much superior to the later Greeks and Romans." I momentarily veered off course to say, "The person who tackles the sexagesimal system will receive extra credit." Nobody giggled this time, a sign that I could resume the lecture.

"They had a twelve-month lunar calendar based on observation of stars, planets, and constellations, so their knowledge of astronomy was astounding. Almost everything we have today can be traced back to the Sumerians six thousand years ago. Choose from these subjects, or get my approval for one of your own."

James Spooner raised his hand, and I shuddered. Every semester some smart-aleck student reads outside the curriculum, trying to make the professor look dumb. Spooner was it for now until somebody more repugnant came along. His name made an easy mnemonic because he was a fat kid, so it was easy to envision him "spooning" ice cream into his wide mouth. I pretended not to see his hand, but he kept it up until all eyes focused on it. I had no choice but to let him speak.

He arrogantly lowered his head, both chins doubled on his neck as he looked at me under bushy eyebrows. "Did Sumerians understand the 2012 date and precession of the equinoxes?"

I should have switched roles. I should have asked him to come up and explain it to the class. I could even have told the truth and said, "Mr. Spooner, I don't know what you're talking about." But hindsight is my best quality, so my pride answered, "I'm glad you brought it up, James. That topic is scheduled for another class period."

Now I'd done it. After class, I fled to my office, locked the door, and sat down at my computer, muttering to myself "precession of. . . uh . . . wait." My bag held an article on the subject. I whisked the rumpled papers to my desk and smoothed them out. The title was still readable: "Precession and the Maya, by Dr. M. Howard." It began as a scholarly thing with terms like "orbital plane," "ecliptic," and "polarities"—stuff I hadn't heard since the last Star Trek movie. "Precession" seemed to be an astronomical term describing the earth's toplike wobbling rotation, which makes constellations appear to move, one after another, over a period of roughly 26,000 years. The equinox part was harder, having to do with the "westward movement along the ecliptic relative to the fixed stars, opposite the motion of the sun." My forehead would soon be etched in a permanent scowl if I continued to read.

In a flash from my memory banks, I realized that the author of this blather was here at my university. Brushing the magazine aside, I reached for the faculty phone book to look up M. Howard in the Astronomy Department. Nothing. Scanning up, I saw Hovorda from linguistics, Hovard in astronomy, Houton in math, Holt in . . . *Wait . . . Hovard?* One letter off. On impulse I called the number .

A deep male voice answered. "This is Dr. Hovard."

"My name is Dr. Howard from the Archaeology Department. I'm looking for the author of an article in . . ." I turned the magazine over. ". . . *Astronomy Review*. Would that be you?"

"Yeah, that's me."

A hit on the first try. "I wonder if I could come over and discuss it with you."

"Sure."

The walk across campus brought me to the astronomy department. Inside, a Foucault pendulum swung from a line attached to the high, domed ceiling. I watched, mesmerized, as the pendulum hit a pin, illustrating the rotation of the earth. I had to force myself to push away and find Hovard's office. The door was open, but I knocked anyway. He looked up and smiled to approve my entry. He was middle-aged, slender, with olive skin, dark hair, and a mustache that circled his mouth to create a goatee. When we shook hands, his grip was firm. In a smooth, low tone he invited me to sit. If the guy got tired of astronomy, he could make a good living as a TV announcer. I explained my need for his help.

"One of my students," I said, "has challenged me with an astronomy term I don't know, and I'm struggling to understand it. Precession of the equinoxes."

He smiled slightly. "Did you check with the astrology department?" *The man is testing to see if I know the difference between astronomy and astrology.*

"There isn't one," I answered.

"Too bad," his mustache went crooked as he gave me a half-smile. "Astrology was a science long before astronomy."

What's with the astrology talk? "Doesn't astrology use stars to tell the future?"

"It's used that way today, but anciently—"

"Wait a minute," I interrupted. "If precession uses astrology to tell fortunes, I'll leave, and we can both save time."

"Precession of the equinoxes is legitimate in both fields. Ancient civilizations tracked the slow movement of constellations to keep time, and precession allowed them to do it on a cosmic level, covering almost 26,000 years. So when you ask if they could tell the future, they knew when an eclipse would occur a thousand years ahead, and when an age began and ended."

"Do astronomers use precession today?"

"No. We determine the center of the galaxy, track supernovas, and measure gamma ray bursts. We don't need a clock in the sky. We wear it on our wrists. But Mayans were obsessed with time-keeping and used precession."

"How did they track something that takes 26,000 years?"

"Who knows? A Greek astronomer named Hipparchus described precession in about 150 BC, but the Mayans were using it at least 3,000 years ago."

Hovard is delusional. Be polite, Matt. "Excuse me, Dr. Hovard, but the Maya are dated between AD 200–900, so how do you figure—"

27

"You're talking about the classic Maya," he patiently explained. "The people before them also calculated precession."

"Do you mean the Olmecs?"

"I believe that's the name they've been given." Nonchalant self-assurance was attractive on him, like a movie star lighting a cigarette while bullets fly around.

I decided not to let it distract me. "Do you have evidence the Olmecs tracked precession?"

"They used a calendar covering a 26,000 year cycle. That's not a coincidence."

"If you're referring to Stela C at Tres Zapotes," I challenged, "a few bar-and-dot numbers do not constitute 26,000 years."

"Would you accept evidence from Izapa?"

I was ahead of him on that one. "I assisted in a dig at Izapa." I tried to be respectful. "We didn't find anything resembling a calendar."

He settled into his chair as if he'd just won a chess game. "It was all around you in the landscape." I almost expected him to say "checkmate." My astonishment must have shown because he sounded pleased. "The whole site is designed to align the December solstice sun with the dark rift in the Milky Way when the precession cycle ends. Olmecs used the site until they disappeared. The Maya took over to keep the parts moving until the end date, when the calendar stops."

"And the end date is . . . ?"

"December 21, 2012."

"That's pretty precise."

"Maybe not. Linguists who translated the calendar narrowed it to that date, but if they forgot to consider the zero year, it'll be 2013."

"Why zero?"

"We're still on a Christian-centered calendar, even though politics changed it to 'Before the Common Era' and 'Common Era.' There's a year '0' that has to be factored in. If it wasn't . . ." He shrugged his shoulders.

"So it could be a year off."

"It could be thirty-four years off."

I leaned back in my chair. "Can you dumb that down for me?"

"Not really."

"Try. I'll grasp what I can."

"We assume the length of the year has never changed, always 365.25 days a year. But Olmec calendars, adopted by the Mayans, were based on a year of six Baktuns, or 360 days. Current calculations could be off by 5.25 days a year, which means the dates we've translated are too far in the past."

He picked up a calculator, saw my blank face, and said, "If the current era—"

"—The fifth one that we're in now." I had to demonstrate a little knowledge on the subject.

He nodded. "If it began in 3080 BC, not 3114 BC as presently determined, then the end date is 34 years later."

My brain tried to process this, but it was slow. Since I made no comment, he took the opportunity to add more complex minutia. "To make matters muddier, there's evidence in Palenque that the Mayan calendar was changed and updated during the AD 700s." My eyes glazed, but Hovard didn't notice. "Inscriptions at Palenque are based on a 365.25 day year and wouldn't match the Olmec calendar anymore. So those dates would be off by twenty-four years."

I held my arm up, like a student with a question. "Regardless of which calendar is used, the Mayan culture isn't old enough to observe precession, and the Olmecs," I used my best professional tone, "date from about 1500 BC to 100 BC, still not enough time to record changes in the sky that take 26,000 years to complete. Where did the Olmecs get precession?"

He bobbed his head sideways and shrugged. "That's a problem for archaeologists."

I matched his head move. "Fair enough," I said, and then rebounded to the important question. "Whether the date is 2012 or 2036 or 2046—"

"Add 2060," he interrupted. "Newton calculated that one."

I ignored the statement. I couldn't afford a diversion. "Regardless of the date, what exactly could happen?"

He leaned forward, hands folded on the desk, and stared at me before saying, "Most people don't like hearing it."

"I asked for it."

He sat back again and took a breath. "Our solar system will align with the galactic equator, which could hit us with maximum mass and gravity. No one knows the effects . . . yet." *Ah, the drama thickens.* "There could be a magnetic field reversal, geophysicists call it a pole shift. Einstein suggested the possibility. It's happened before. The old North Pole was close to Wisconsin. If there's another shift, the new North Pole could be near Brazil."

My response turned flippant, almost rude, but Hovard deserved it. "So we'll make new maps."

He became the picture of patience. I got the feeling he had tried to explain this before. "If the shift is rapid, a few days or hours, we could have a global superstorm with 300-mile-per-hour winds, lasting months. The planet would be sandblasted."

I added my reaction. "Then what could survive except cockroaches?"

He indulged my attempt at humor. "Penguins and polar bears," he said. "Extreme northern and southern areas wouldn't be affected as severely."

Thanks for that information." I rubbed the back of my neck in relief. "You had me worried there for a minute."

Hovard's reply was quick and sharp. "Stay worried. Even if reverse polarity takes years, the result would be global climate change and shifting sea levels. The stress on the planet would aggravate earthquakes and volcanoes."

"If it's slow, we can see it coming and get ready, right?"

"We're seeing it now: changing weather patterns, hurricanes, tsunamis. Ocean liners report at least one rogue tidal wave every month."

"How bad can that be?"

He leaned toward me in emphasis. "There aren't enough sand bags in the world to hold back the Gulf of Mexico when it comes up the Mississippi." *He's serious about this.* "On top of that," he added, tipping back, "about the time of the 2012 winter solstice, the sun will enter its sunspot cycle." Hovard eyed me quizzically. "Do you understand sunspots?"

"It's not my area of expertise," *Sunspots . . . bad news . . . affect the earth . . .* "I remember they're dark blotches on the face of the sun, and a guy in the 1980s discovered they come in cycles of eleven and a half years."

"I'm impressed," he said. I felt like a student whose professor had offered lavish praise. I hoped he wouldn't notice my blush as he said, "What most don't realize is that sunspots are connected to solar storms that affect Earth's magnetic field. NASA predicts the next solar storm will be 30–50 percent more powerful than anything we've seen before. A big solar storm could disrupt the electrical power distribution grid. Communication and travel would stop."

The talk had turned heavy. I tried to lighten it. "Does that mean my computer won't work?"

Hovard, deep into doom and gloom, announced, "Nothing will work."

"You've got an interesting sense of humor," I shot back. "How can a person tell when you're joking?"

He closed his eyes a moment and then opened them. "It's no joke. Keep any old tube-type equipment you have. It should be okay, if you can find electricity." We stared at each other before he said, "Do you want more?"

"You have my attention."

"Coronal mass ejection from the sun could fry us."

I pursed my lips for two seconds. "Well, Dr. Hovard," I finally said, "I think you've told me more than I need to know."

One side of his face lifted in his crooked-mustache smile. "You asked for it, Dr . . . uh . . . I'm sorry, I didn't catch your name on the phone."

I was thrilled to change the subject. "It's Dr. Howard, just one letter away from your name. Which brings me to your article." I placed *Astronomy Review* on the desk, embarrassed at the obvious lack of respect it had received at my hands. The thing was crumpled, rumpled, and underlined. "I'm assuming the name 'Howard' was a typographical error and should have been 'Hovard'."

He shook his head several times. "They printed an apology in the next issue, but I've never seen a professional journal make a mistake like that."

"Well, it's caused me some trouble. I ended up going to Chichen Itza in your place."

Dr. Hovard's face froze. "You went to Chichen Itza?"

"The Barbachano family sent an invitation for the fall equinox, plus plane tickets, hoping to discuss an article I'd written. When I got there, we realized it was your article they'd read." I laughed nervously. "You can imagine how . . ." I looked at his wilting mustache and misplaced my thread of thought.

The man's voice dripped disappointment. "You got an invitation meant for me?"

I did a backstroke to soften the blow. "I'm terribly sorry I took your vacation. It was an accident. I'm sure they'll invite you next time."

His response was quick but quiet. "That day was a one-time event. It won't happen again."

"Look, if it makes you feel better, I totally missed the snake show. They dragged me inside the pyramid to see an old man who spoke gibberish about how I had to warn my people." I rolled up my sleeve and stretched my left arm out for him to see. "And they put an indelible mark inside my elbow. I'll have to surgically remove it."

He sat like a zombie, mesmerized by the design. I looked down to find the picture was darker, the pattern forming the head of an animal.

"The Age of the Jaguar," he said to himself. Then he turned to me, his eyes steel-hardened. "You've been marked."

Big surprise. I'm so glad you told me.

I wanted out of this conversation loop. "You can consider yourself lucky you missed the party. Like I said, I'll have to have the tattoo cut out professionally."

"It won't come off," he said as he rearranged his desk, putting pencils in a tray. "You'll have to do the work."

"What work?"

He gathered books and articles like there was an outside force of energy moving him to action. "What did they tell you to do?"

"The old man said to warn my people."

"Then you'd better do it." He stood, moving to a bookcase and sliding the books on the shelf.

"This is crazy," I protested. "I don't know what's going on or how I got into this mess. It should be *you* wearing this mark."

Dr. Hovard turned to me and leaned on his desk. "Do you know how long I studied to understand this phenomenon?" His voice was low, almost dangerous. "Can you guess how much I wanted to be part of it?" He stood taller, resentment hovering in the air between us. "And *you*, who know nothing . . . you, who wish to forget it all, YOU have been given the mark in my place."

Mayday. Retreat. "Look, I just came to ask if you'd explain precession of the equinoxes to my students—"

"Get out."

Stunned, I stood to speak my final appeal. "I'm sorry. It was a mistake!"

"There *are* no mistakes."

FOUR

I fled the crazed astronomer who was still randomly redistributing items in his office. My shoes padded on the gray floor tiles, not slowing as I passed the Foucault pendulum. It had been a long time since I'd been ordered out of a room—fifth grade, in fact, when I threw up on the floor and it splashed on the surrounding students. The teacher had commanded me to see the school nurse, with a hint of sympathy in her voice. There had been no kindness in Dr. Hovard's tone.

I rolled my sleeve down to hide the darkening picture inside my arm, the profile of a three-inch square jaguar head, complete with fangs. Maybe I could sue the Barbachano family for elbow defacement. Until then, I had classes to teach, precession to learn, and a daughter to win back. As for Dr. Howard, I truly wished he had the jaguar tattoo, only I wanted it on his nose where he couldn't hide it in a long-sleeved shirt.

Sitting in my office, I hunkered over Howard's precession article, trying to find something I could use, looking for what had caught the interest of the Barbachano family.

Western science sees time as a line, relentlessly moving forward. The Mayans understood it as a cycle with natural rhythm. They believed time repeated itself. If they knew what happened in the past, they could tell what would happen in the future.

Been there, heard that, I thought.

The Mayans did not elaborate about what would happen in AD 2012. However, there has been no end to the forecasts by modern interpreters. Even NASA predicts that 2012 might be a record year for sunspots. According to one report, the next cycle will be 30 to 50 percent stronger than the historic solar max of 1958, when the Northern Lights were seen as far south as Mexico.

I didn't need NASA's opinion. Ten minutes with Hovard was enough to scare the wits out of me. I flipped a few pages to find he had waxed occult.

Currently, the vernal equinox is in Pisces, at the cusp of Aquarius. We are presently finishing the Age of Pisces and will soon enter the Age of Aquarius . . . .

Music rolled into the background of my brain. "This is the dawning of the age of Aquarius, dum dum de dum de dum . . ."

It is suggested and supported by a growing weight of evidence that the precession cycle was recognized at least during the age of Taurus, perhaps even back to Leo, as represented by the Sphinx at Giza.

A sidebar displayed constellation signs and the estimated years it took for their precession, give or take.

Leo: 10800 to 8640 BC
Cancer: 8640 to 6480 BC
Gemini: 6480 to 4320 BC
Taurus: 4320 to 2160 BC

Aries: 2160 BC to 0
Pisces: 0 to AD 2160
Aquarius: 2160 to AD 4320

My eyes skimmed the rest of the information and then shot back to constellation Leo. Did Hovard actually connect it to the Sphinx? What science fiction paperback did the man use as his source? The Sphinx is officially dated at 2500 BC, not 10,000 BC. I tossed the article across the room, disgusted that Hovard could mingle mainstream astronomy with astrological signs and still get published. "Nobody was measuring precession during the age of Leo," I yelled at the air. "Primitive people spent all their time staying alive."

New background music entered with the Bee Gee's singing, "Stayin' Alive."

The phone jangled, jerking me out of Hovard's fantasyland. A man's voice spoke in my ear—the same melodic voice that had ordered me out of his office an hour earlier.

"Dr. Howard?" it said.

I spoke his name timidly. "Dr. Hovard?"

"I can explain precession to your class next week."

His repentance was matter of fact, without apology, but I grabbed his offer like a stick in stormy seas. We arranged his guest appearance with the understanding he would limit his lecture to precession, leaving out all the prattle about the end of the world, and we parted on good terms. Precession and my Sumerian class had been taken care of. Now all I had to do was figure out where my sweet daughter was and get rid of her evil twin.

That evening, dinner was a study in still life. The only sound effects were the grating of forks on plates. It was so quiet we could hear each other swallow and then set our glasses down again. The silence finally drove me to fill the empty space with unrehearsed words and unconsidered consequences.

"All right, Marisa!" I slammed my fork to the plate. "Since you're so unhappy, I'll take you back to China. Maybe you can find your *real* mother." We faced each other across the table while I maintained a front of anger. Marisa's face resembled a stone carving—enigmatic, unreadable. Her reply was more surprising than my brain-dead suggestion.

"Okay," she said.

Well, rats. That wasn't the reaction I'd expected. Gearing into automatic, I pushed from the table, stormed to the office, breathed deeply, and returned in full control with her adoption papers, which I gently placed in front of her.

"It's all yours," I said coldly. "Find a time, an itinerary, and a price to China that won't ruin our Christmas savings." Smugly rejoicing at my accidental brilliance, I exited the room in a breeze of power, knowing the project would keep her busy all year and come to nothing.

The next morning I hid the wretched jaguar under a long-sleeved shirt, making a mental note that I couldn't keep alternating the only two I possessed. I spent the drive to campus wondering where I could get long-sleeved shirts in Arizona, and by the time I entered my pottery dating class, I believed the dark animal on the inside of my arm could be seen through the sleeve fabric. Self conscious, I held my left arm stiffly at my side. When Sumerian literature rolled around, I'd forgotten the mark and waved my arms as usual, punctuating comments and ideas. We were studying the seven creation tablets of the *Enuma Elish,* named for its opening words:

> *Enuma elish la nabu shamamu,*
> When in the heights Heaven had not been named
> *Shaplitu ammatum shuma la zakrat,*
> And below, firm ground (Earth) had not been called

The translation continued:

> Naught but primordial Apsu, their Begetter,
> Mummu, and Tiamat, she who bore them all;
> Their waters were mingled together.

No reed had yet formed, no marshland had appeared.
None of the gods had yet been brought into being,
None bore a name, their destinies were undetermined;
Then it was that gods were formed in their midst.

The five-thousand-year-old tablets had been discovered in the library at Nineveh in 1876. The myth was also found in Assyria and in the Mesopotamian cities of Kish and Uruk. The *Enuma Elish,* popular in its day, tells the origin of the gods, the world, and humans. The story starts like a child's dark fairy tale, written by an ancient Brothers Grimm.

Tiamat, the water dragon and goddess of birth, and Apsu, the begetter, produce young gods who create too much noise in heaven and Apsu decides to destroy them. Word gets out and one of the offspring kills Apsu. Tiamat creates an army of monsters and dragons to avenge the death of her consort, putting fear into the lesser gods. Along comes Marduk, the hero, who volunteers to get rid of Tiamat. The young gods are happy, have a banquet, and get drunk. This gets us through the first three tablets. Now our class faced part four. The violence alone would make Hollywood blush. I had been forced to read it for my undergraduate studies and now, twenty years later, I taught it in my Sumerian/Babylonian literature course. We had reached the grim part where Marduk gathers weapons from the other gods and attacks Tiamat.

They swayed in single combat, locked in battle.
The lord spread out his net to enfold her.
The Evil Wind, which followed behind, he let loose in her face.
When Tiamat opened her mouth to consume him,
He drove the Evil Wind that she close not her lips.
As the fierce winds charged her belly,
Her body was distended and her mouth was wide open.
He released the arrow, it tore her belly
It cut through her insides, splitting the heart.

Having thus subdued her, he extinguished her life.
He cast down her carcass to stand upon it.
The lord trod on the legs of Tiamat,
With his unsparing mace he crushed her skull.
When the arteries of her blood he had severed,
The North Wind bore it to places undisclosed.
Then the lord paused to view her dead body,
That he might divide the monster and do artful works.
He split her like a shellfish into two parts;
Half of her he set up and ceiled as sky,
Pulled down the bar and posted guards.
He bade them to allow not her waters to escape.
He crossed the heavens and surveyed its regions.

"Dr. Howard?" A timid female voice echoed in the classroom.

"Yes, Gina?"

"What is this story about?"

"It's the Sumerian creation story and the war of the gods for supremacy. Marduk won. After he killed Tiamat, the gods gave him kingship over the universe, and he used Tiamat's body parts to create Earth."

"It's gross. Is there a deeper message somewhere?"

"The translators haven't found one," I told her.

"I don't like it." She squirmed in her chair. "You keep telling us the Sumerians were civilized, but this isn't a good example."

"The *Enuma Elish* is disturbing," I agreed. "Take a deep breath. We have three more tablets to cover."

A male hand shot up, and I nodded consent for Jake to speak.

"I think it's cool," he enthused.

"Thanks for your opinion, Jake. Take a deep breath. You get to enjoy three more tablets." I turned to the class. "By the way, Dr. Hovard from the Astronomy Department will explain precession of the equinoxes on Friday. There's a lot to cover, so everybody take a deep breath before then."

If I could peek into the future, I wouldn't be taking deep breaths, I'd be hyperventilating.

FIVE

10.13.2004 / APPOINTMENT TO REMOVE JAGUAR TATTOO

Dr. Martin made an effort not to laugh when he saw the tattoo on the inside of my arm, probably thinking it was the evidence of an older woman trying to recapture her reckless youth.

He did, however, allow himself a slight grin. "What were you thinking?"

I replied evenly, "I was unconscious at the time."

His grin faded as he regarded me with suspicion. I could read it in his eyes—he was wondering if I'd dabbled with hallucinogens.

I looked directly into his eyes. "Can you get it off?"

He examined my arm, donned a head microscope to peer closer, and then poked and pulled at the skin.

"Hmmmmmm," he said. "Huh," he remarked. "How long have you had this?" he asked.

"A little more than a month."

He removed his headgear and scrutinized me, scratching his well-shaved chin. "It's not a tattoo," he explained. "It's more like a birthmark. You say you don't know how it happened?"

"I was comatose."

"Did you agree to it?"

"No."

"Did you know the people who did it?"

"No."

He studied me as if I were hiding something.

I had to admit, it seemed unlikely I'd be with people I didn't know who chloroformed me and printed a mark inside my elbow. However, I wasn't willing to give details, so he finally said, "I haven't seen anything like it."

Dr. Martin sent me to a lab where they scanned my arm and promised to send the results to the doctor. He called back a few days later.

"Matt," he said, concern in his voice, "your tattoo is too deep to remove without serious damage to your arm. It reminds me of a *naevus flammeus* or port-wine birthmark, except those are a red stain in the skin and yours is a black picture. I rarely suggest getting a lawyer, but in your case, I think you should take your assailants to court. I have no doubt you'd win."

Sure I would, until I told the jury about the Old One and my assignment to warn my people—whoever they are. The court would mandate a trip to a psychiatrist.

I searched in vain for long-sleeved shirts, finally becoming desperate enough to enter a second-hand shop with an old-fashioned bell on the door that announced my entrance. The store was the kind of eclectic place that might appeal to underground hippies still clinging to the golden days of Sonny and Cher, who never trusted anyone over thirty. Jewelry racks and baskets hung from the ceiling. Misogynistic shoes with pointed toes, designed to cripple women, stood in cubicles stacked artistically in corners. I moved to the racks of clothes in the center of the room where I quickly found two shirts with long sleeves, one the size of a Barbie doll, the other a middle-age spread. I took the big one and walked to the cash register, pounding the circular bell for assistance. A cute old thing emerged from behind a curtain of purple beads and walked to the counter. Her wrinkled face sat on top of a size-two body, dressed in Levi's, high heels, and a turquoise puffy-sleeve blouse. Her mid-length hair, also puffy, was bleached a honey-blonde. When I'm an old woman, I want to look like her. Even now, at forty-something, I wouldn't mind looking like her.

She spoke in a deep gravelly voice, which was surprising considering her small size. "Hi, honey," she said. "Did you find what you want?" Maybe she smoked too much.

"I found what I need," I amended, placing the shirt and my wallet next to the register.

"You know, sweetheart, this isn't your color."

"I don't care about color." I put my credit card in front of her. "I want cover."

She picked up the plastic and pushed it through her little machine. "If you'd lose twenty pounds, darlin', you wouldn't need cover."

Stupid skinny person. "Thanks for caring," I retorted, signing the paper and dropping my card in my wallet. History proves that style shifts. In modern times we are held prisoners at the whim of the media. A hundred years ago I would have given her advice on how to *gain* weight.

There's a stranger inside me who pops out when I lose control. It's like a *Three Faces of Eve* thing. Against my will, Eve surfaced and explained to the skinny lady why I needed a cover and that it had nothing to do with poundage. "I've got a tattoo," Eve's voice came from my mouth. "I have to hide it until it can be removed." To prove myself, I pulled up my sleeve to show the jaguar. My Eve persona is stupid.

The little lady stared at my arm for two seconds before grabbing it for a closer look. "Is this what I think it is?"

"That depends," I answered, "on what you think it is."

She examined my face. Slowly I loosened my arm from her grip as she announced, "You bear the mark."

I dropped my head in frustration and then abruptly raised it and glared at her. "Who are you? How do you know about this?"

"Honey, I'm nobody. I just dabble in the art. But you share something with the great ones, people in the past who left the warning: Merlin, Mother Shipton, the Sibylline Oracle, Nostradamus—"

I turned nasty. "All a bunch of phony fortune tellers. Do you have a crystal ball in the back room?"

She didn't respond to my rudeness. "Sweetie, listen to me. You have a heavy responsibility."

"Right." The word tasted bitter. "I'm supposed to carry a sign that says, 'The end of the world is coming.' "

"It is." She straightened, which still meant she had to look up at me. "But walking around with a sign won't help. You have to tell people what to do."

I pulled myself together to say calmly, quietly, and in a normal voice, "I don't *know* what to do. Why don't *you* tell them?"

The cute little old lady studied me, slowly shaking her head. "You're marked for a reason, but on the surface I can't see why."

I recognized the insult. "You and me both, kiddo. It was a mistake."

Her gravel voice grated against my ear. "There are no mistakes."

"Lady," I said, nettled beyond endurance, "I don't want to be rude, but I'm going to be rude. I'm a real, live, bona fide, card-carrying scientist. I don't study Nostradamus." I pivoted on one foot, strode through the belled door, and took eight steps toward my car before remembering the long-sleeved, wrong-color blouse I'd paid for. Marching back to the shop, I opened the tinkling door to see the smiling little lady holding out a bag with pink tissue peeping from the top. Grabbing it from her hand, I stomped outside.

"Have a nice day," she called cheerfully.

When I got home, I pulled the used shirt from the bag for laundering. A lavender 8½ x 11 inch paper floated to the floor. I picked it up and made the mistake of reading it.

PROPHECIES OF THE END TIME OF OUR DAY

Mayan Book of Chilam Balam, Jaguar Priest, AD 1160s, Katun Thirteen

This is a time of total collapse, when everything is lost. It is the time of the judgment of God. There will be epidemics and plagues and then famine. Governments will be lost to foreigners, and wise men and prophets will be lost.

The Sibylline Oracle, AD 380, Book Four

These things in the tenth generation shall come to pass. The earth shall be shaken by a great earthquake that throws many cities into the sea. There shall be war. Fire shall come flashing forth from the heavens and many cities burn. Black ashes shall fill the great sky. Then know the anger of the gods.

Fifth Century Myrrden (Merlin), England

There will be an astrological ending. The planets will run riot.

Mother Shipton, England, 1500s

When pictures look alive with movements free
When ships like fishes swim beneath the sea
When men outstripping birds can soar the sky
Then half the world deep drenched in blood shall die.

Letter from Nostradamus to King Henry II of France, June 17, 1558

The great Empire of the Antichrist will begin where once was Attila's empire, and the new Xerxes will descend with great and countless numbers. . . . This will be preceded by a solar eclipse more dark and gloomy than any since the creation of the world, except that after the death and passion of Jesus Christ. And it will be in the month of October that the great translation will be made, and it will be such that one will think the gravity of the earth has lost its natural movement and that it is to be plunged into the abyss of perpetual darkness. . . . In the spring there will be omens, and thereafter extreme changes, reversals of realms and mighty earthquakes. . . .

45

Nicholaas Siener van Rensburg, Afrikaaner prophet, 1900s

I see a great war, fast and furious. It will be fought mostly from the skies. I see weapons that we have not even dreamt of. Germs will cause sickness. Electric rays will devastate the earth. . . . This will come to pass when the ice starts melting.

Kolbrin Book of Manuscripts: Egyptian-Celtic wisdom preserved in Great Britain.

Men forget the days of the Destroyer. Only the wise know where it went and that it will return in its appointed hour. It raged across the Heavens in the days of wrath. . . . These are the signs and times which shall precede the Destroyer's return: A hundred and ten generations shall pass into the West and nations will rise and fall. Men will fly in the air as birds and swim in the seas as fishes. Men will talk peace one with another, hypocrisy and deceit shall have their day. Women will be as men and men as women, passion will be a plaything of man.

These are things said of the Destroyer in the old records. Read them with a solemn heart, knowing that the Doomshape has its appointed time and will return . . . and in accordance with his nature, man will be unprepared.

On the opposite side of the page were more quotes that I refused to read. In pen at the bottom were the words, "Call when you're ready," followed by a phone number.

"Not in this life," I said, crumpling the paper and dropping it in a wastebasket.

There would come a time when I would need that purple paper.

On Friday, Dr. Hovard breezed into my Sumerian class ten minutes late.

The man was shameless.

"I'm a Scorpio," he announced while setting up his star charts. "Dr. Howard is a Cancer." He turned to me apologetically. "I looked up your birthday." His grin sparkled through the mustache on his handsome face.

I offered an artificial smile as I sat at a desk in the back of the room. "I'm fine with that, as long as you don't announce the year."

Hovard turned to my class. "Is anyone here a Pisces?"

A girl on the front row raised her hand.

"Your constellation," he announced, "has been the sun's backdrop for roughly 2,125 years, the age we're in now. Is anybody an Aquarius?"

Another girl raised her hand but only halfway.

The man was intimidating.

"Your sign will be pushing Pisces out of the way soon, and Earth will begin its new age of Aquarius." He searched the faces of my students. "I need a Sagittarius."

A young man lifted his hand. One of his eyebrows was raised quizzically. I could read the boy's thoughts because they were also mine: *Dr. Hovard is a nutcase.*

"Aha!" Hovard said with enthusiasm. "Did you know your constellation is the best physical marker we have of our galaxy's center?"

The bewildered kid shook his head as Hovard explained, "We've never actually seen the center because dark matter hides it, but we believe there's a massive black hole there that keeps our galaxy glued together." He saluted the boy and then spoke to the class. "Another way to locate our galactic center is to get some good binoculars, go outside at midnight on or around December 21, and look straight up. The dark area where no stars are shining is the galactic plane—sort of like its equator. That's the direction our star system is going. We are approaching it at a 60-degree angle. Every year, the darkness will get bigger until 2012 or so."

Students were giving each other furtive looks, as if to say, "What's this guy doing here?" I slunk down in my chair and debated whether to throw up, like I had in fifth grade, which would effectively cut the class short.

"Does anyone here not know his zodiac sign?" No hands, which meant they either knew their signs or didn't understand the word *zodiac* and were too embarrassed to admit it. "The point is," Hovard said, "even though we call ourselves 'scientific,' we still know which constellation we were born under. We've inherited the information from the deep beginnings of antiquity. For us it's only a game. To them it was a giant clock in the sky."

A clock in the sky. The concept held me captive, like a key to treasure or a clue to mystery. Hovard's melodic voice crooned on about the zodiac and constellations marching across the heavens like sentinels in a parade.

The man was hypnotic.

He finally introduced the agreed-on topic. "The earth not only rotates," he said, "it wobbles, making it appear that the twelve constellations slowly take their thousands-of-years turn behind the sun. Earliest civilizations noticed the change was one degree every 71.6 years. Ancient mathematicians calculated that the entire cycle would take about 26,000 years to complete, give or take a few hundred. And that, class, is called 'precession of the equinoxes.'" He smiled at Miss Pisces and Miss Aquarius. They melted under his charisma like teenage girls at a rock concert.

The man was a manipulator.

A male hand shot up. "I'm an Aquarius too. When will we enter that age?" The class thermometer warmed under Hovard's spell.

"Nobody agrees," Hovard said without a trace of apology. "Newton thought the beginning of Aquarius would be 2060, others said 2080. What we know for sure is that the sun will still be inside the constellation of Pisces until after 2012."

James Spooner slowly raised his hand in a calculated trap. I didn't know how to shut the dreaded kid up. Hovard would have to deal with it on his own.

"Let me get this straight," Spooner began. "Because the earth wobbles, it appears that every 2,125 years or so, a constellation takes its place behind the equinox sun, and the ancients called it an 'age.' "

Hovard smiled and nodded. "Excellent recap," he said, oblivious to what Spooner was capable of.

The fat kid continued. "And it takes 26,000 years for all the constellations to get their turn and that's precession of the equinoxes."

Hovard kept smiling and nodding. I cringed in anticipation as Spooner carried on. "Pisces will move and Aquarius will take over, but not until after 2012."

Hovard shrugged his shoulders.

Spooner had a look of evil triumph as he pulled his trump card. "So why is 2012 so important?"

The kid knew about 2012. I lowered my head, anticipating disruption and a barrage of questions about the end of the world. Hovard didn't flinch an eyelash as he said, "The winter solstice happens every year on December 21. In the year 2012, at 6:48 AM, our solar system will line up precisely with the center of the galaxy on the galactic equator." Hovard turned from Spooner, arms spread in excitement as he strode in front of the room like a Shakespearean actor. "Last time the earth was in this position was 26,000 years ago. The whole world," he moved his arms to take in everyone, "should have a party to celebrate the event. The best place to see the center of the universe will be 30 degrees north, so if you can get to the Pyramid of Giza on December 21, 2012, you'll have a perfect observation platform." Some students scribbled notes as fast as their pens could wiggle. Others sat like frozen zombies in rapt attention. "And," Hovard concluded, "we all need to write a journal entry to tell what it was like to live at this historic time."

Spooner raised his hand again. Hovard recognized it but said, shaking his head in honest regret, "You and I have a date to talk after class." He turned back to the room of students. "Right now I have to prepare you for a quiz on the ancient Sumerians and their use of precession."

The word *quiz* refocused the class like lightning. Students opened notebooks and searched for pens. I sat straighter in my chair, relieved at how nicely Spooner had been silenced. Of course, now I'd have to write a quiz, but I had to hand it to Hovard.

The man was a skilled teacher.

When class was over, I watched my mesmerized students gather around Hovard, asking questions. He charmed the girls, joked with the boys, and walked from the room in deep discussion with a certain fat boy who followed him like an adoring puppy. Hovard had tamed James Spooner. I sat glued to my chair in the back of the room as if I'd just seen an award performance.

The man was magnificent.

Later, like a teenager with a crush on Elvis, I checked Hovard's faculty bio.

The man was married.

SIX

11.02.2004 / VOTE

I shouldered my civic duty and stood in line at the credit union where I'd tossed my meager ballot into the box two years ago. Controversy had tainted the campaign from TV ads to billboards, and Election Day was guaranteed to draw droves. When the line reached the door, a small written notice told me my district had been moved to the new high school. Somebody at the city must work full-time on changing the venues every two years.

At the school, each parking space was full. Abandoning my car on the road, I walked to the line outside the door, taking my place behind a man studying architectural plans. He rolled them in scroll fashion, bumping my shoulder in the process.

"Excuse me," he said.

"Not a problem," I assured him, wishing I'd brought a book to keep me occupied.

We inched into the building and began a Disneyland weave through barriers set up for crowd control. The woman in front of my architect struggled with a whining three-year-old. I watched her until our eyes met, passing the empathy that mothers share. "Enjoy this stage," I told her. "It stops being fun when they're thirteen." She smiled wanly and pulled the kid on her hip. My lower back hurt from the mere memory of that move.

The line shuffled, dragged, scuffed, and hobbled. The man adjusted his paper again, barely missing my head. I noted his appearance, roughly five foot eight, stocky build, with big hairy hands and the ruddy face of a construction worker. We edged past the glass doors into the main building as the mother's struggle heightened. Suddenly, her child emitted a full power scream, echoing off the high ceiling. "I give up," the woman said through clenched teeth. As she turned to leave the line, the kid kicked the man's arm, sending his papers to the floor. The woman trampled them in her rush to exit.

"Don't step on it!" he cried out, too late. I bent to help him salvage his designs, noticing that the plan in my hand showed a long, horizontal cylinder with recessed, hinged bunks, kitchen cabinets, and long tubes leading outside the structure. Attached at a ninety-degree angle was a second, smaller cylinder with rungs inside like a ladder. The entire design resembled a submarine.

"This is interesting," I said, expanding the roll for a better view. "Where are the windows?"

"There aren't any," he said, reaching for the paper.

I turned to avoid his retrieval, holding the plans slightly above me. "It doesn't look like a standard house. Is it underground?"

"Yes." His big hand forcefully jerked at his plans, and I gracefully let go, hoping to give the impression that I'd freely given it to him. My neck stretched to follow the paper back to his possession. "How far underground?"

He hesitated before saying, "Sixteen to twenty feet."

I cocked my head, eyes wide and eyebrows arched in an invitation for him to enlighten me. I'd helped save his precious plans. He owed me conversation. "This is fascinating," I enthused. "Could you explain it to me?" I displayed my patented little-old-lady smile and added, "Better to know than guess."

He only had a few choices. He could answer my obnoxious questions. He could try to change the subject, which would require too much energy. Or he could exit the line and return later when I was gone.

He analyzed his options before saying, "It's an underground shelter."

"Like a bomb shelter?"

"No. A bomb shelter is short-term—only a few weeks." He folded the plans and put them in his briefcase, probably so I couldn't grab them again. "This one is designed for comfortable, long-term living."

"How much 'long-term living?' "

"About two years. Everybody's different."

"Why would someone need to live underground for two years?"

"I don't know." I gave him a three-second stare until he added, "Honest. I don't know."

I let it go. "Why the round shape?"

"A flat roof could collapse under eight feet of dirt."

"Is it made of concrete?"

"Concrete is too expensive. We use a corrugated steel culvert. It accommodates the earth's movements and also makes a sort of 'Faraday cage' to protect electrical devices from EMPs."

The only thing I hate more than sounding stupid is being stupid, but I had to ask. "What are EMPs?"

"Electromagnetic pulses, the latest war technology. If an enemy detonates an EMP bomb in the air, it would fry all computer-based technology and shut down the power grid."

"You're joking."

"If it's a joke, I'm laughing all the way to the bank."

Keep smiling, Matt, and keep him talking. "How long have you been building these shelters?"

"More than twenty years. We've figured out every square inch of space: water and food storage, ventilation systems, chemical and biological filters, sanitation, cooking facilities, wiring. We've thought of everything. Our shelter will protect against tornado, hurricane, earthquake, winter storm, even nuclear disaster." He raised his briefcase as a visual aid. "These plans are getting tweaked for a customer who needs—" He stopped. " . . . some changes."

"How did you get into this business?"

He breathed a little "I give up" sigh, finally realizing he was stuck in line and couldn't get rid of me.

"I had a friend working for the government," he began, "who had clearance for one of the big shelters, but his family couldn't go with him. So he asked me to design a private place."

"What big shelters?" *Pay attention, Matt. This is new stuff.*

"Okay, look," he said. "I already have more work than I can handle, so don't repeat this." I nodded agreement. "The government has underground bases to use as shelters for themselves and people they consider valuable. Every state has at least two or more. There are rumors that new construction may be a mile down."

I heard the words but they didn't register. It took a while to brush the shock away. "Why do they need a shelter that deep?"

He shrugged. "They're expecting something big."

"I don't remember my congressman voting to pay for underground cities."

He produced a knowing smile, the way a kindergarten teacher considers the innocence of a child. "They've got a *black budget*," he said. My face must have gone blank because he gave a small laugh and continued. "You don't really think they spend $30,000 on a toilet, do you? The toilet costs $500 and the rest goes into the "black budget" to be used on pet projects. The federal budget is $500 billion a year. And $310 billion builds and stocks their cities."

I let the information find a place to sink in, but there was already too much debris in the way. First, I was confused about why the government would waste $500 on a toilet. Then I grasped the enormity of the fact that a "black budget" was being used to build underground cities for elected officials while the rest of us would be upstairs getting nuked, fried, frozen, starved, mashed by asteroids, washed by gamma rays, and flooded with EMPs.

I returned to the conversation. "Have you seen the official shelters?"

"Nah. Only politicians have clearance. After them, the invitations go to doctors, lawyers, and scientists. The list probably includes Hollywood celebrities and a few construction engineers."

"Do you know where any of these shelters are?"

"Groom Lake, of course, in Nevada . . . also Los Alamos. The one in Virginia is called Mt. Weather and has a tunnel to the White House. There's an eighty-square-mile facility beneath the Denver Airport. Everything is connected."

"Do other governments have these shelters?"

"I've been told Russia has an underground base in the Ural Mountains, paid for with American dollars that were supposed to be used to dismantle nuclear weapons. Northern Mexico has one. Sweden is in on it. There's probably more, but I'm an outsider. I build for the guys without clearance. They don't talk much."

"What do governments know that the rest of us aren't aware of?"

He leaned his head to the side to crack his neck. "I don't ask questions. I just build their shelters."

"Next, please." A woman's voice jerked us into realizing we'd made it to the front of the line.

The man walked to the table, wrote his name, took his ballot, and disappeared behind a curtained booth. When it was my turn, I checked his signature—Jeffrey St. Paul—and wrote the name on my hand. My head buzzed with the old birthday chant we used as kids: "Heavy, heavy hangover thy poor head. What do you wish this person?" No doubt about it, my head was in a hangover. As for the wish, I hoped all those rats in Congress would get hit with an EMP and not be able to travel to their underground cities. Better yet, I hoped they'd make it inside but wouldn't be able to get out.

I think I punched the wrong holes in the voting booth.

When I got home, Marisa was on my computer.

"Hey, babe," I said pleasantly, hoping for a good connection. "I need the computer for official research."

She didn't look at me. "I'm doing official research too."

I maintained sweetness and light. "I promise not to lose your place."

She moved in sullen slowness to slip from the room as I minimized her travelogue on China and typed "Jeffrey St. Paul." He was hiding in plain sight with a logo that blazed across my screen: "Hazard Shelters for Every Emergency." The pictures showed steel culverts in a variety of sizes, with the ten-foot diameter structure highlighted as most practical. It took thirty minutes to read through the text. The price, prohibitive in the extreme, didn't include bunks, cabinets, or little luxuries like food and water. Whoever ordered one of these things paid a hefty price for peace of mind. A shudder raced down my back as I considered being buried alive in a container with ten feet of dirt on top of me.

The computer trapped me in its maze of information as I investigated "Mt. Weather" and "underground cities." When the Internet reports started including stories of lizardlike aliens living under the Denver Airport, I shut the computer off. Marisa returned to find I'd lost her site and flounced from the room before the words, "I'm sorry" could reach her ears.

Oh well.

Hazard shelters dogged my thoughts every day for a week, interfering with my classes. I needed to discuss the underground cities with someone who didn't have to be brought up to speed. This eliminated everyone but Hovard.

Reluctantly, I wandered to the astronomy department and knocked on his door, hoping he wouldn't be there. I was still chaffing at the adolescent way I had searched the faculty bios to see if he was married. I hadn't acted like that for . . . well, a long time.

He was in.

Rats.

"Dr. Hovard," I said as I walked through the door.

He rose from his chair behind the desk. "Dr. Howard," he said, with one nod. I hadn't had a man stand for me in . . . well, a long time.

We both sat.

I cut straight to my purpose. "I've had an unnerving experience and I want to run it by you."

He nodded.

"At Chichen Itza," I began, noting his cringe, "I told Mr. Barbachano he should notify governments and let *them* warn people. He said the governments already knew and had plans to save themselves. I didn't believe him, especially about my government."

Hovard's mustache moved down, evidence of a grimace.

I continued the story. "On Tuesday I stood in line to vote behind a man who builds family-size shelters for government officials who can't go to one of the hundred or so underground cities. What do you know about it?"

Hovard didn't display a blink or shred of shock. "I've heard rumors."

"Can we . . ." I amended the words. "Can I run down these rumors to substantiate them?"

"Not unless you want to disappear."

"Isn't that a little paranoid?"

His melodic voice weakened me. It was good to be sitting down. "Loose lips," he quoted, "sink ships."

"Very clever," I said sarcastically. "I think I'll call my trusted congressman."

Hovard's humor turned ugly. "Your congressman doesn't care about you. He's the guy who votes himself a raise every year, who's left you with a dead Social Security system while he has a lifetime government pension and health care. He doesn't want you to know that the President isn't the only one who has a safe place during a disaster."

The truth in his words was heavy on my shoulders. I allowed myself thirty seconds to rant about it. "What infuriates me is how they advise us to hunker down in our basements, surrounded by books for protection, while *they* spend our money on underground cities."

He lowered his voice, probably so I'd lower mine. "Do you know how deep the cities are?" His moderate tone calmed me.

"The new ones are supposedly a mile down." His right eyebrow lifted at the dubious possibility, and I hurried to add, "That's third-hand information."

Hovard pondered the statement, shaking his head. "What are they preparing for?"

"Aren't they getting ready for the 2012 date?"

"No." He said the word absently, as if he were busy figuring out the real motive. "They're not paying attention to ethereal threats."

"Ethereal?" The word stopped me cold. It took a while to form a response. "Are you kidding?" I sat taller in the chair. "You practically paralyzed me with fear over calamities that can happen when we line up with the great equator in the sky. Now, you're discounting it. What do *you* think will happen on December 21, 2012?"

"Personally?"

"That's a good start."

"Nothing. I think the day will come and go without a whimper."

All the color in the room suddenly imploded into gray, a precursor for my explosion into red. "Then *what*,"—I pulled my sleeve up to display the jaguar tattoo—"is *this* about? What disaster am I supposed to tell people to prepare for? You and the Barbachano family have jerked me back and forth over the end of the world, and now you tell me nothing's going to—"

"Wait, wait, wait." Hovard held both hands up to ward off the verbal blows of my fury. "There's a window of seventy-two years, from 1976 to 2048, based on a conjunction of the zenith sun with the Pleides over Chichen Itza. December 21, 2012 is the center date, but Earth is in the zone right now. We've already got strange weather, earthquakes, tsunamis, and melting ice poles. The real violence could be after the 2012 date, when we'll see drastic weather changes, super volcanoes, 300-mile-per-hour hurricanes, and world-shaking earthquakes. People need the message now to get ready. But the day itself will probably be a fizzle."

I stood from the chair. "I want out. I can't live like this."

He leaned forward and softly spoke my name. "Matt . . . it's no coincidence that you went to Chichen Itza in my place. Other people don't stand in a voting line and hear that the government has underground shelters. Nothing happens by chance. When you're ready, the information will find you, and you'll know what to do."

I leaned across his desk, still angry, my hands splayed on top as a prop. "What's your part in this?"

"I don't know."

"Will you tell me if you find out?"

"That depends on what I'm supposed to do."

I pushed the chair away with the back of my knees, and it crashed to the floor. Without apology I swirled, stepped over the chair legs, and walked out of his office. In a quick return, which ruined my dramatic exit, I peeked around the door and said grudgingly, "Thanks for teaching my class."

I huffed out again as he called behind me, "No problem."

The handsome, brilliant astronomer was wrong. Everything was a problem.

My Sumerian class finally finished the *Enuma Elish*. After Marduk decapitates, guts, and decimates Tiamat in Tablet Four, he returns to clean up the mess, throwing half her corpse into the heavens, using the rest to create Earth, her spittle in the clouds, rivers from her tears. Nice imagery. In Tablet Five Marduk creates a twelve-month calendar, with the heavenly bodies as a clock. In Tablet Six he sacrifices a lesser god, using the bone and blood for the creation of humanity to serve the gods. Tablet Seven expounds the greatness of Marduk and his fifty names, among them "Nibiru," a star that crosses heaven and earth.

As the translation put it:

Nibiru is the star, which is bright in the sky.
He controls the crossroads, they must look to him,
Saying: "He who kept crossing inside Tiamat without respite
Shall have Nibiru as his name, grasping her middle.
May he establish the paths of the heavenly stars,
And may he shepherd all the gods like sheep.

Whatever name he used, I was weary of him. But Marduk, posing as the star Nibiru, wasn't finished with me.

SEVEN

11.10.2004

Marisa and I had our own version of a solar storm. She called me a kidnapper, and I took away her TV privileges. It was random punishment, inflicted in anger at the moment, having nothing to do with her crime. That night I lay awake, trying to think of something reasonable I could have said or done, since now I'd have to monitor the TV. As it turned out, Marisa spent every spare minute at the computer, desperately searching for a cheap trip to China. I almost felt sorry for her.

Almost.

The next day an envelope, addressed to Dr. M. Howard, appeared on my office desk, postmarked Mexico.

It felt sinister.

The envelope sat there like a spider, waiting for my move. I knew touching it would bring a Pandora's box of regret. My hand might swell, turn black, and ooze rotting flesh onto the paper. Finally I made a surprise attack, ripping it open. Two pages fell from the shredded envelope. The first was a letter.

Dear Dr. Howard,

You are invited to the New Fire Ceremony at Izapa on

Saturday, November 20. The rite was last performed in 1507. Enclosed is a ticket to Tapachula. A colleague will meet you at the airport and take you to the sacred site for instruction. The ceremony takes place at midnight. Accommodations are included, and we will return you to the airport on the 21st. We hope this letter finds you well.

The Barbachano family.

The second page was the plane ticket. I dashed off a hand-written retort on their letter:

I may learn slow, but I learn good.

No thanks.

—Dr. Matt Howard

While refolding the papers, a voice inside my head argued, *It's only two days, on a weekend, financed by the fiend family. Go to Izapa. Get away from Marisa.*

I'd done ceramic dating in Izapa as a grad student. The ruins sit near the city of Tapachula in the Mexican state of Chiapas, on the border of Guatemala. Ancient Olmecs designed the place for religious rituals as early as 1500 BC. Mayans took over from 50 BC to AD 1200. Aztecs used the site before the Spanish conquest. The whole story could be told by broken pottery. I love my job.

Arrangements for the Mexico trip slid into place like greased pigs at a trough. Even Marisa cooperated and agreed to stay with a friend. I crammed my maroon daypack with water, food, and extra clothes and then fell into a Continental Airlines seat late Friday night.

DAWN / 11.20.2004 / TAPACHULA INTERNATIONAL AIRPORT

They don't call it "red eye" for nothing. Even the pilot slumped over the wheel after landing. With my pack slung over my shoulder, I bypassed baggage to the exit, where a girl held a small sign written in black marker.

"Dr. Howard?" She addressed me before I'd read the sign.

"That's me," I replied. "Who are you?"

She was all business, no friendly smile. Maybe it irked her to get up before dawn. "I'm your driver to Izapa." The girl stood under five feet, a pretty little thing—her smooth, light olive skin contrasting with green eyes, hinting at some influence from the north. Short, dark brown hair held red highlights, probably store-bought. We locked eyes for an instant before she said, "The elders thought you'd be more comfortable if a woman came." Her English was straight off the streets of any city in America.

"The elders are wise." I grinned. *Woman, indeed, this girl is seventeen at most.* "I'm nervous at coming alone, even though everyone knows where I am." *Nobody knows.* "How did a sweet young thing like you get involved with the crazy Barbachano family?"

She produced an artificial smile and pushed open the glass doors, leading to humid air. "It was easy," she said. "My name is Evangeline Barbachano."

As first impressions go, I'd thrown a gutter ball. "Where did you pick up native English?"

"I was born in Watsonville, California. That's where I live."

"Where do you fit with the Chichen Itza people?"

"It's a big family . . . seven sons, four daughters, lots of relatives. I'm one of thirty-two cousins." Evangeline led me through the parking lot to a square SUV, navy blue, sitting high on its wheels. The back, stuffed with groceries held in boxes and plastic sacks, showed the name *Hummer*. I wondered where the family got money to send plane tickets to strangers who might not use them, and buy ugly, expensive cars. Evangeline touched the door, which automatically unlocked. "Izapa," she said, "is twenty-eight kilometers away."

I'm old. I'm behind. I'm embarrassed to ask. It took a few mental twists to figure that twenty-eight kilometers is about seventeen miles. By then we were well on the road toward the Guatemalan border, where Izapa lay in ruins.

We talked in polite generalities. She had come to help with the ceremony. I explained my interest as an archaeologist, leaving out my elbow jaguar. I asked about the New Fire Ceremony.

"Aztecs did it every fifty-two years," she said. "The Spanish invasion stopped it, but Mayan elders say we have to do it again for the last time."

"Why are Mayans doing an Aztec ceremony? And why is it the last time?"

"Everything has to be restored before the end, even Aztec stuff. When Earth enters *Xibalba be*, the cycles are over. The New Fire won't be done again."

"*Xibalba be*?" I'd heard the term from the Old One.

Evangeline defined the term. "It's the road in the sky to the center of the universe. The sun enters it in 2012." She turned her head to study me. "You should know this."

My smile didn't offset her distrust. "I'm glad you can explain it."

Her head moved quickly back to the road. "Not me," she said. "One of the elders will take you through initiation." I didn't like the word *initiation*. It smacked of sorority hell week, eggs dripping from the hair, crawling across campus in flour sacks. I scratched my jaguar tattoo. Suddenly, fear struck. Maybe they planned to sacrifice me on one of their altars. Then I laughed out loud as common sense told me I was too old, too fat, and too perverse to be of use to the gods.

"Why are you laughing?" The girl's tone held suspicion.

"Nothing important," I said. "I just realized I forgot water." *I'm producing lies already. Bad sign.*

"The elders will give you food and water."

I don't think so, sweetheart, I thought. *Last time your family offered me a drink, I woke up with a headache and a tattoo.*

A small sign at our left directed us to the ruins of Izapa, and my teenage chauffeur whirled the car onto a bumpy road. We slid to a stop in dust and gravel, under a tree hiding an adobe hut. She exited the car, ignoring me, and moved to the back to unload groceries.

I followed her. "Do you need help?"

Her answer was curt. "No. Wait here."

It was the end of a budding friendship. *Oh, well.*

I leaned against the car. The sun hadn't risen yet and already the hot moist air weighed heavy. A burly man in loose Levis and a red and white checked cotton shirt held the screen door for Evangeline and then let it slam as he walked toward me. He'd covered his head with a striped, faded red kerchief, tied in back. His close-set eyes had bags large enough to pack, and a gray stubble of mustache hinted at the probable color of his hair. A necklace of animal teeth, brown with age, hung lopsided against his shirt. Two deep creases from both sides of his nose to the corners of his mouth were not the result of smiling. "I'm Carlos," he snapped. "You're Dr. Howard. We didn't think you'd come." His English was perfect.

"Neither did I," I stammered. So far, this trip wasn't worth the plane ride. I could have stayed home and been insulted by Marisa. The big man, seven inches taller than me, looked down to say, "We have a lot to do. We start now."

I fitted my day pack over my shoulder. He shook his head. "Leave your bag."

"I think I'll take my own food and water."

"We have bottled water."

"I'd be more comfortable if—"

The man walked away. "Fine. You have to carry it."

I jogged behind him until I caught up.

"So, Carlos, where are you from?" No answer. I probed. "Watsonville, California?"

He stopped and turned to me. "Dr. Howard, you're here to learn what the ancients knew about the cosmic calendar. I'm assigned to get you through the basics. The ruins cover one and a half square miles. It's going to be a long, hot day, so save your energy."

I dropped to the rear, and we marched across fields, past farmhouses and cacao trees. Most of Izapa is on private land, with farmers struggling to make a living. Squealing pigs scattered as we stepped over a wire fence. Two monuments stood inside the enclosure.

"Wait," I said. "I'd like a closer look. Those stelae have—"

"You're not a tourist today," Carlos threw back at me. He lifted one leg over the pig fence, then the other, and strode on, not looking back to see how I fared. I was tempted to feign helplessness but decided a pig sty wasn't the best place. While we hiked in silence, I contemplated the irony of sacred Mayan standing stones ruling over pigs.

Only a small portion of Izapa has been excavated. Mounds of various sizes sprinkled the ground, unstudied and unappreciated. Sweat formed under my maroon pack. The land opened into a large plaza, its freshly mowed lawn surrounded by carved, upright stone stelae, protected from weather by green tin roofs. Carlos stopped in front of one, six feet tall, four feet wide, surrounded by multiple barbed wires. A flat altar sat like a step in front.

"This is Stela Five in Group A," he stated flatly. "Your people say it was carved in 300 BC and gave it a meaningless number. Stela Five is where the ancient priests began their training."

I recognized the famous carving, with a central tree, seven people surrounding it, birds in the tree branches, and water running through its roots.

"The Tree of Life Stone," I announced. "Nobody agrees on its meaning."

He stiffened. "Your scientists are fools," he said, "wandering in their own darkness, never searching for truth among those who know."

Tread lightly, Matt. "I'm here to learn from those who know." *That ought to soften him.*

It didn't. He spoke his words to the stone. "Stela Five is a long, complicated narrative of those who migrated here. It tells their origin, their trials, and their names." Carlos walked away.

"Hold up," I called to him. "That sounds like something I should know."

The grouch turned and stared at me, apparently deciding whether I was worth speaking to. "Priests needed twelve days for the initiation at Izapa," he finally said. "You have one. There's no time for background." He continued walking to the next stela and then waited for me.

"Fine," I grumbled through my teeth, ambling to his side. The carving showed an upside-down alligator, mouth closed, tail straight up branching into a tree. Across from the tail a large, elaborate macaw bird sat on a perch. I turned to the miserable Mayan for an explanation.

"Stela Twenty-Five," he abruptly said. "The alligator is the Milky Way. When the mouth opens, it becomes the dark rift that leads to the black hole in the center of the galaxy." He pointed to the bird. "This is Seven Macaw, the false ruler of the last Age. Soon, the true Galactic God and father of the Hero Twins will take his rightful place and Seven Macaw will fall from his throne." He looked at me sideways. "Do you know the Hero Twin story from the *Popol Vuh*?"

"I do," I said, my nose held higher in the air to look up at him. "The Hero Twins journeyed on a dangerous adventure to rescue their father from Seven Macaw and—"

"Good. Then I don't need to waste more time." The great lump of a man left me standing in the weeds. He walked past two other monuments, waving his hand toward them. "These give more details." Carlos traversed the plaza to a group on the opposite side, his loose Levis flapping with each step. I trailed behind. "Over here are Stelae One, Two, and Three." He pointed to the middle rock. "In Stela Two, the Hero Twins shoot Seven Macaw out of his perch to make way for their father, One Hunahpu." I stooped to examine the altar, etched with a frog. Carlos moved away, and I rose to follow.

He stopped at a carving of a long-lipped god walking on water, wearing a basket on his back. The Mayan's voice drilled his statement. "Here is where priests learned the rotation of stars around the pole. The cycle on the stone is clockwise, but priests entered the rock to observe the stars moving counterclockwise. Truth can be seen when the priest is inside the stela." He advanced to the next monument.

"Wait a minute." My growing irritation became obvious. "I have questions." His mouth tightened, but I stood my ground, and he stopped to listen, a small miracle. "Explain how they got inside the stela."

Carlos raised his hands in frustration, moving his big feet toward the center of the plaza where one stone with its green roof sat isolated from the rest. When I got there, he spoke. "This is Stela Six. What do you see?"

"It's a frog," I said, "head back, wide mouth holding someone in a canoe."

"What else?"

Why does he suddenly want my input? "On the frog's back," I said, "are several dots releasing smoke or a mist . . ." I stopped.

It hit.

"They used drugs," I said quietly. "The initiate had a triptamine vision from frog venom."

"Toad venom," Carlos corrected. "And mushrooms. All the stelae have altars in front for psychoactive substances. Your experience here would be quicker if you—"

"Sir," I said with enmity, "the last time your family gave me a drink," I pulled up my sleeve to reveal the jaguar, "I was left with this."

He saw it and looked away. "The young elders agree an older female isn't capable of the work. You know nothing and can't learn. It's a mistake."

I wound into a tight little spring of anger. "Well, they marked me anyway, and I'm all you've got. Besides," I heard myself quote the hated words, "there are no mistakes. I came a long way to learn what you're supposed to teach me. So start talking, Carlos, or I'll find another elder. I don't have time for toad venom."

He stood still and stared at me, one eye squeezed to a slit, as if focused on something far away. "Come on, then," he said with a new tone to his voice, maybe respect, maybe resignation.

We climbed a grassy mound that faced north. To my left stood three tiers of a temple platform, the flat top cleared of blocks. On the right was a smaller version. We were on the largest mound, holding center place in Group A. Before me a volcano floated above a misty cloud bank. Carlos motioned for me to sit on the slope and close my eyes. His voice drifted across my face, sinking, dipping, luring mind from body.

Go back five thousand years to a black sky full of stars. Face north, to the volcano Tacana. Seven Macaw slowly rises from the mountain top, revolving over his perch, finally dropping in the west. He rules for 2000 years, until there's a change in his pattern. Breathe the smoke of the Galactic toad for enlightenment. Gaze into the polar zone. The sky shifts, time opens, stars speed through their cycles. Nights chase each other until the moving spheres blend into rings of light above you. Seven Macaw rises and falls, over and over, rising, falling, swinging away from his center, away from his throne, no longer on the summit of Tacana but sliding east down the slope of the mountain . . ."

My eyes jerked open. "I get it," I said. "The bird, Seven Macaw, is the Big Dipper, circling its perch, the star Polaris. Five thousand years ago it appeared over the peak of Tacana but now, because of precession, it rises over the eastern slope of the mountain. Seven Macaw is literally falling off its throne. Group A keeps track of it."

The big man moved down the slope. "You're ready for Group B."

Straining to stand against the hill's gravity, I chased Carlos to the end of the plaza, and we exited Group A.

EIGHT

Heat boiled down from the sun to rise again—sizzling from moist grass, creating poached archaeologist. My short hair stuck to my forehead, producing rivulets of salty sweat. I pulled a bandana from the pack and tied it, Carlos-style, around my head, wishing I'd brought an umbrella for shade.

Group B greeted us with three pillars in the center of the plaza that had stone balls balanced on top. The pillars resembled soldiers, arranged like the stars in Orion's belt. They would look menacing at night, as if they were warriors waiting for attack orders. I circled the six-foot-tall central pillar, obviously meant to measure the sun in the sky.

The ancients were serious about their gnomons," I said to Carlos. "A stick in the ground could have told them when the sun overhead didn't cast a shadow. Why carve rocks?"

Carlos stood next to the sculpted giant. "The site had to last through the Fifth Age to deliver its message."

I couldn't stop my sarcasm. "It was nice of people thousands of years ago to worry about us."

"Survival of the species," Carlos grimly said, "is always 'nice.' "

The stelae of Group B pictured gods reaching zenith in the

heavens: a quetzal bird flying straight up to the Milky Way; One Hunahpu sitting in a canoe with arms outstretched to measure the galaxy; One Hunahpu in the mouth of a frog, symbolizing the dark place in the Milky Way, leading to alignment with the galaxy at the end of time.

An hour of studying faded carvings brought us to a large hill called Mound 30, eroded into a pyramid of dirt. Several trees grew from the mound's sides, but a hard-packed trail still revealed where ancient feet had climbed to a temple on top. In the middle of the path, a single atrophied bush eked out an existence. With the entire hill to choose from, it had settled at the hardest spot to grow. The stupid bush was the logo for my life.

We sat under one of the larger trees to eat lunch in the shade. Opening my pack, I offered a peanut butter sandwich to Carlos.

He wrinkled his nose. "No thanks," he said. "They'll bring something."

I scanned the dirt mounds. "I don't see a taco stand."

"They know we're here."

I shrugged and pulled a hot, soggy sandwich from its plastic bag. The thing, twelve hours old, dripped with melted honey off the crust, brown peanut butter leaching through the bread. Carlos watched, amused. If I'd been alone, I would have tossed the sandwich and eaten an indestructible protein bar, but pride prevailed. I bit into the nasty wet bread with pretended enthusiasm and, through teeth filled with brown goop, asked, "Sure you don't want one?" He shook his head.

A man dressed in white pants and shirt, sandals on his feet, appeared at the bottom of the mound and climbed toward us, carrying a tray of fresh tortillas. He handed it to Carlos, the two men nodded at each other, and the white-clad fellow retreated.

Carlos held the tray under my nose. "Sure you don't want one?" The stupid man hadn't smiled all day, but now he grinned broadly, making his nose-to-mouth creases into gullies.

"I'm fine," I lied. I still didn't trust these people.

We ate while I reviewed the lessons in Groups A and B.

"Group A," I said, my mouth stuck in warm peanut butter,

"concentrates on keeping track of Seven Macaw, the Big Dipper." Carlos wrapped a tortilla around white cheese while I pretended not to notice. "Group B," I proceeded, "measured the zenith of the sun at various times of the year." I drank warm water which tasted flat and saline.

"Here," Carlos said, "is where the beginning of the Mayan calendar was computed."

I knew the date. "That would be August 13, 3114 BC."

"Only for your people," Carlos made the distinction. "And they can't agree. For us, it is Four Ahau, Eight Kumku."

"Yeah, I know," I told the big man. "I looked it up. Is anything else measured here?"

He replied with his usual annoyance. "The zenith of the Pleiades constellation."

"What for?" I couldn't find the Pleiades if I searched, much less calculate when it was directly overhead.

Carlos rested his arms on bent knees. "Do you know about the New Fire Ceremony?"

"Should I?"

He lowered his head and then lifted it and took a deep breath. "The Aztecs watched the Pleiades to keep track of their fifty-two year epoch, like your century. It was a big celebration. The nation broke everything from the past and swept it away. All fires were put out. When the Pleiades reached zenith, priests started a sacred new fire to celebrate continued life. People took the fire to their homes and began the next fifty-two years."

"Sounds like a nice tradition," I said. "Do I get to see that at midnight?"

He hesitated. "Yes, at midnight."

Something wasn't right, but I couldn't put a name to it, so I kept talking. "Do you have any other traditions that I should know?"

He deliberately clinked the ice in his glass, producing music in my ears. Ice water isn't typical in Mexico. For reasons I couldn't yet figure out, Carlos wanted me to eat and drink their stuff. That fact gave me courage to resist.

72

He gulped the water and then answered my question. "Venus is very important to my people. The observatory at Chichen Itza is designed to track it."

"We know that, but nobody knows why." Carlos went rigid, so I did a backstroke. "Please explain it."

He softened slightly. "My people consider Venus the sister of Earth. In fact, the beginning date of the Mayan calendar is called *The Birth of Venus*. We worry when Venus moves between Earth and the sun. The transit is rare, takes about 6 hours, and happens in intervals: 8 years, 121.5 years, 8 years, 105.5 years, 8 years, another 8 years, and then it starts over." The rat looked over at me and leisurely bit into his cheese tortilla. "It goes like that forever." I rummaged for a protein bar while Carlos finished his story. "Venus warns Earth of change," he said. "A disaster happens several months later."

I sighed. "It's always disasters with you guys. Give me an example."

"A Venus transit happened in June of 1518, just before Cortez landed." He spoke without emotion.

"That wasn't a natural disaster," I protested.

"Catastrophes can also be made by man. The Spanish destroyed us more completely than an earthquake."

I bowed my head in agreement. "Fair enough. Tell me another time Venus did a sun dance."

He was quick. "1883."

I didn't catch the significance of the date and cocked my head like a questioning dog.

He answered with irritation, as if the information should be at the front of my brain. "Krakatoa erupted."

His statement stopped me for a few seconds while I reviewed my history. The explosion pushed Earth into a mini ice age, ash from the volcano circling the globe several times. "Okay," I said. "That counts as a catastrophe." I crunched a dry protein bar. "When does the Venus transit happen again?"

The big man adjusted his head covering. "It already did, last June. The egress predicts what part of the world is affected."

I laughed. "It's a shame you guys got me instead of the astronomer. He'd know what you're talking about."

"An egress," he clarified, "is when Venus leaves the face of the sun. Last June the egress could be seen in Europe, Africa, the Middle East, Asia, and Indonesia. The warning could apply to any of them." He shrugged. "Or all of them."

I smiled at the quaint superstition. "Then, according to Mayan tradition, Venus has warned those countries to get ready for something drastic in a few months. I'll be watching the news."

The man wiped his hands on a small, wet towel, placed his tray on the sloping grass, and lifted himself to his feet. "I'll meet you at Group F." He trotted, partly slipping, down to the plaza.

I figured I'd made him angry. "Wait . . . what about C, D, and E?"

He ignored me, turned right at the bottom, and vanished around Mound 30. I grudgingly wiped my hands on the grass, threw my garbage on his tray, and slid down the big dirt hill. By the time I'd rounded the mound, the Mayan's strong legs had put distance between us on a path following the Suchiate River, the boundary between Mexico and Guatemala. He must have sprinted to get that far.

My pack felt like a large wet cat attached to my back, digging its claws into my shoulders. With the river on the right and Izapa on the left, I hiked through the tropical sauna, passing farms, stumbling over pebbles, and losing Carlos.

NINE

The jungle unwrapped Group F like a scene from a children's pop-up book, framed with mounds, monuments, and stelae. I entered its page through a passage between two dirt hills. A green plaza spread like a carpet in front of me. To the right stood a three-tiered viewing platform, six stairs leading to the upper level, which was large enough for a crowd of fifty tourists. The lower levels could have held an additional hundred. Directly east stood a higher structure with thirteen stairs leading up to a stage and a stand of trees behind acting as a backdrop. This would be a perfect place for farmers in the area to produce a show for hundreds of tourists and supplement their incomes. I planned to share that idea with Carlos if I ever found him again. At the moment, I was the only living thing that moved at Group F.

To the left was a ball court with a hundred-foot-long by thirty-foot-wide playing field. Raised viewing platforms spanned its borders. I walked east along the length of the silent ball court, once packed with crowds cheering, chanting, and shouting for the players. Two teams would fight to hit a rubber ball through one of two rings embedded in the sides of the court. The ball could not touch the ground, and players used any part of the body except hands and feet. The stakes included beheading a team captain. Some scholars say the loser was killed, others insist the winner made a worthier sacrifice. Personally, I don't see the incentive in winning if you lose your head.

Monuments interspersed themselves along the route, but my goal was a stela at the east end, its tin protective roof glinting in the afternoon sun. Reaching it, I stared at the picture of a man standing over a dead bird god: Seven Macaw—the Big Dipper—had been conquered. Beyond the trees, I imagined One Hunahpu, the sun, rising at the winter solstice.

I turned around and an electric buzz of shock passed through my gut as I saw Carlos sitting on a short stone stool at the west end of the ball court. The sun behind him created a halo of light surrounding his outline. I walked toward him, stifling a loud laugh when I got closer. The elder looked ridiculous, squatting on a low throne with his legs splayed out. A head carved in the rock was settled in his crotch, as if he were giving birth.

"Carlos," I said. "What are you doing?"

"Welcome to the birthplace of the Mayan calendar and the 2012 end date."

"Are you supposed to be having a baby?"

He spoke sternly. "This is a sacred throne depicting the birth of the Solar Deity."

"I apologize." I spread my arms wide to emphasize regret and then dropped them to my sides. "What does Group F measure?"

"The galactic center. The womb of the Great Mother. For a thousand years, mysteries of the galaxy were taught here with ritual so it could be remembered. To the north, Seven Macaw's fall began around 1000 BC. He moved south, from Tacana toward another volcano." My eyes followed his hand upward as he pointed past the east end of the ball court. "Tajumulco," he boasted, "the highest mountain in Central America, final destiny of Seven Macaw."

Hovard had been right. The clock in the sky hangs on the

horizon at Izapa. In an epiphany of understanding, I spoke to Carlos. "This is where precession could be measured, and the end date computed."

Without moving his head, his eyes rolled up to glare at me, nearly disappearing under his brows. "Isn't that what I've been telling you all day?" He didn't give me a chance to respond. "The primary message of Group F is in the ball court."

I viewed the long, narrow playing field as Carlos continued. "The priest who sat here observed the dawn of the solstice sun. Witnesses sat behind him."

Twisting, I saw six round stools behind the little throne Carlos was giving birth on.

"They watched," he said, "to see if the sun and the Galactic Mother would join. For eight thousand years, the Milky Way Mother remained high in the sky. Twenty-two hundred years ago, she was closer, 30 degrees above the solstice sunrise. Ancient priests calibrated a calendar to predict the future union of First Father and Cosmic Mother. The Long Count Calendar—"

"—the one that's 26,000 years." I had to slip that in.

Carlos closed his eyes and kept talking. "The Long Count has five number places and works with the Tzolk'in calendar that has been followed for untold ages. When the date reaches 13.0.0.0.0, the union of Father and Mother will be achieved. The Old Ones left stories and legends—"

"Like One Hunahpu and Seven Macaw."

He persevered. "Stories and legends to help us understand that the rising sun and the dark area of the Milky Way—"

"—which is *Xibalba be*—"

The annoyed man slowly turned his head my direction. "Stop." It was a command.

"Sorry."

He sulked before saying, "The rising sun and the dark area of the Milky Way is the event awaited for 26,000 years." He paused for me to interrupt, so I didn't. He continued. "One Hunahpu and the Galactic Mother are soon coming together."

I couldn't resist. "On December 21, 2012."

He nodded solemnly. "At 6:29 in the morning, here at Izapa."

"And the ball game?"

"It's a metaphor that warns us of the end of both our Fifth Age and the Great Cycle. The goal ring represents the womb of the Great Mother, the place where time begins and ends. When the ball goes into the ring, new birth occurs. The game of time is over."

"Two strikes against Earth," I said cheerfully. "It's Double Jeopardy."

He shook his head like a teacher disgusted with a student. "You have no respect. I don't understand why you were marked."

"I'm sorry." I wasn't. The whole womb-birth thing seemed juvenile. "What does the ball represent?"

"The head of One Hunahpu," he said. "The sun."

I asked the central question. "And when the sun and the womb of the Great Mother meet . . . ?"

Carlos struggled from his squat position on the throne. "Time's up." He headed into the jungle.

Confused, I followed the big man out of Group F and back to the jungle path, scurrying to keep up. "Are you talking about time finishing at 2012?"

"No," he called behind. "Our time for your training is up. People need to prepare for the ceremony. I'm taking you where you can eat and rest until later."

"How very thoughtful of you," I said. *What's wrong with this picture? Since when has Carlos been nice to me?*

The sun sat almost on the horizon. We tramped for fifteen minutes through a south field, stopping at a small whitewashed adobe hut in a grove of cacao trees. Weeds grew against the screen door. I imagined snakes slithering through the tall growth. Carlos pulled the entry open, and we entered a sparse, one-room hut. A single bed with a cotton cover occupied the center of the room, which also held a washstand with a ceramic bowl full of water and a chair by the door.

"This is the guest room," Carlos said with a straight face. "I assume you'll want to eat dinner from your pack. Get some sleep. I'll come for you when the time is right. There's an outhouse behind the trees." He lumbered out the door and was gone. Darkness collapsed the day like an accordion.

I got real nervous.

First checking the bed for critters, I sat on it with my maroon bag on my belly, searching for survival gear. There was enough water. I'd lugged it around all day, cursing and complaining. Now I felt like I'd pulled a fast one on Carlos and the gang. It's good to be self-reliant. Miserable . . . but good.

Sitting cross-legged on the tiny bed, I ate three protein bars, keeping the crumbs on my bandana so I could shake them outside. I'd also packed two apples, now bruised. I ate one with a melted chocolate bar, saving the other apple for breakfast in the morning, if I lived that long. I didn't brush my teeth, afraid to use the water in the bowl. A visit to the outhouse brought me scurrying gratefully back to the hut. After pushing the washstand against the door for security, there was nothing to do but lie down. The last time I'd slept in a hut in a third world country, I got head lice.

The sound crawled into my ears like ants, quietly unnoticed, until the rhythm popped my eyes open, and I sat up straight. Voices chanted in the distance. Carlos had forgotten me. I tied my shoelaces, ran one hand through my hair, and rushed for the door. My flashlight guided me into the night, revealing safe places to put my feet as I pursued the sound of humanity. When I got closer, against all reason, I switched off my lantern.

The chanting increased by decibels, but the only light came from the stars. When I reached the Group F complex, people were packed against each other. I wound between bodies, finding the six stairs leading to the platform I'd seen that afternoon, its top and sides now filled with swaying natives. I quietly worked my way to a place where I could view the stage as six men climbed the thirteen stairs. They surrounded a seventh man—shirtless, young, his body sculpted in muscles. His brown skin glistened but not with sweat. Most likely it was oil, an anointing of some kind. At the top edge of the stairs a long, flat couch had been set up. The couch had a strange bulge on its right, like a human face staring into the audience. Even without light I knew who it was. Chac Mool, the sacrificial idol at Chichen Itza.

Three men in white, already on the stage, slowly walked to the idol as the first group faded into shadow, leaving the youth on top.

I had a bad feeling.

In the time it took me to breathe once, the three men threw the boy on the couch, one held his feet, another his hands over his head, and the center man raised something blacker than the night and sunk it into the boy's naked chest.

"NO!" It was my voice that cried against the dark. I plunged forward through the people in front. A rough hand from behind covered my nose and mouth, stifling the screams. A male voice whispered brutally in my ear, "Shut up, stupid woman." I understood the words through a heavy accent. "Shut up or I kill you." He tightened his grip until oxygen became my solitary thought. I felt my eyes bulge and I went limp. He moved his hand from my nose, again whispering in my ear, "It is done. Watch or go." I nodded submission, and he lowered his hand, keeping it on my upper arm.

There was sudden silence, the chanting stopped, and maybe even breathing ceased as the three men on top surrounded the body and worked feverishly. Their arms and elbows moved in and out like doctors in a comedy operation done at high speed. The smallest glow of light, like a cigarette a long way off, formed within the circle, radiating against the white clothing of the ceremonial chiefs. They parted, stood behind the body, and raised their arms in victory. One held a bundle of fiber, one an obsidian knife, the third a primitive hand drill that produced the fire spark. Flames in the chest cavity of the victim leaped up to illuminate the faces of his murderers. The crowd went wild.

I fell to the ground, vaguely aware of people moving past me. Someone offered a metal folding chair with one leg broken, and I crawled onto it, my head bowed. When I looked up, people were climbing the thirteen steps with fire bundles to light, giving them New Fire from the boy's chest cavity. My stupor was too intense to think of looking at my watch. It may have taken hours. Eventually, the throng trickled to their homes to keep the sacred fire going for another fifty-two years.

In reality, they would douse the fire and switch on their electric lights.

A presence stood beside me. I glanced up to see Carlos.

He had a chair. "May I join you?" He didn't wait for permission before setting the chair next to me.

"So, Carlos," I said. "Your people learned to measure three cosmic centers: polar, zenith, and galactic. They did it with absolute accuracy. And they went to all that trouble so they'd know the precise time to kill a young man."

"You don't understand," he spoke gently. "The ancients believed the blood sacrifice of the New Fire Ceremony prevented the end of the world for another fifty-two—"

I cut him off. "What kind of . . . thing . . . are you? Your ancestors believed that silly rituals could change the stars, but *you're* an educated man. Nothing you do will change the clock in the sky. You can't wind it up or slow it down, and your cosmic centers will move whether you do a blood sacrifice or not."

His attitude changed to ugly. "We knew you'd be trouble."

"Why did you invite me?"

"Others with authority insisted on it."

I spoke without fear. "I'll go to the police, of course."

"The police were here. One of them stopped you from making a scene."

Defeated, I leaned my forearms against my knees, lowering my head over them. "What do the Pleiades have to do with killing that young man?"

Carlos stared ahead, toward the stage. "The sun-Pleiades

zenith is part of the end of the calendar. It aligns over the Pyramid of Kukulcan in May, but the sun is too bright to see the Pleiades."

"Imagine that." Sarcasm was all I had left.

He didn't react. "We check the Pleiades zenith in November so we'll know that six months later Pleiades and the sun will meet over the pyramid. It's an alignment that only occurs during a seventy-two year period—this time from 1976 to 2048. And 2012 is at the center." *Hovard said that.*

"Big deal." I raised my head. "You can't see it, but you commit murder because of it."

His frustrated sigh could have knocked a bird off its perch. "Are you familiar with the Aztec Calendar?"

"Of course. It's in the museum in Mexico City."

"The center picture is their Sun God, Tonatiuh. His tongue hangs out to symbolize the knife. Outstretched hands hold hearts. Four glyphs around him symbolize the cataclysms that ended each of the former ages."

I spoke dully. "Each one lasting 5,125 years."

The big man completed his message. "The glyph at the center says our age will be destroyed by earthquake. The Aztecs felt they had to do something . . . anything . . . to prevent it."

"Fortunately," my voice sounded vicious, "their barbarism was stopped by the Spanish. Why would you do their grisly ceremony again?"

"It had to be done for the last time in this age. We won't get another fifty-two years." He pointed to the Milky Way, still visible in the sky. "Look how low it is to the horizon. See the dark rift? It leads to the nuclear bulge at the center of the universe, held together by a black hole, hidden from us by dark dust." *Hovard said those words.*

"It's almost time," Carlos announced. "You might as well see the rising sun against the galaxy center."

"No." I shook my head. "I'm sick at what I've already seen."

"You came a long way."

I stared ahead. "I didn't have to pay for it."

He lost patience. "Fine. Stay here and miss it." He stood, picked up his chair, and moved behind me to descend the six stairs. His stroll across the plaza took him to the west end of the ball court.

Mumbling, I trailed behind.

When I sat next to him, he said without turning, "You should be on the throne to get the best view."

"The one that makes it appear that I'm giving birth?"

"That's the one."

"Will you promise not to look?"

His mouth tightened, and I knew I'd pushed too far. I moved to the throne, bent my knees to a squat, and dropped into place.

Staring down the ball court, I could see that the Milky Way was, indeed, close to the horizon. At about 6:30, the eastern sky brightened over the stela of the fallen bird god. Trees prevented a full view of the rising sun, but a brilliant ray shot through the foliage to hit us full in the face. The tin roof of a farmer's shed at our left burst into light, as if on fire. We watched, enthralled, as the sun arced toward the south, not yet aligning with the Great Mother, but coming close. The playing field lit up as if incandescent bulbs were placed along the periphery.

"It's undeniable," I said, loud enough for Carlos to hear. "Izapa was built to show the winter solstice alignment in 2012."

Carlos took a turn at sarcasm. "My people will be thrilled to hear you agree with us."

I let a little time die before saying, "Everything's catastrophic. The Aztec calendar predicts a massive earthquake. Venus brings destruction when it crosses the sun. The Izapa ball court measures the end of the great cycle at the 2012 solstice, and we get a double whammy with the end of the age. Is there any good news?"

"Well . . . ?" he said, his voice trailing off in a question mark. "The world isn't going to end."

I sat on the hard stone, legs spread in birth position. "Then what's all the fuss about? Why am I marked and told to warn people?"

"The sun is born when it enters the birth canal of the Milky Way. Warn your people to prepare for pain. There is always pain during birth."

TEN

Carlos drove me from Group F to the airport in the Hummer. I wanted to give him the silent treatment but I had too many questions.

I stared straight ahead. "Did you know the young man?"

"No."

"Did anybody in the crowd know him?"

"No. Ancient sacrifice was usually a war captive. Nothing personal."

I bristled. "I think it's personal to get killed."

Carlos remained mute until I finally asked, "Why didn't he struggle?"

"We're good with psychotropic plants." The big Mayan showed no emotion, no regret. "He was already in another world."

"How old—"

Carlos broke in. "Maybe you can think of better questions in the time you have."

I kept quiet for awhile and then asked, "If I'd taken your food and water, would it have—"

"Yes. I planned to take you to a good hotel where you'd wake up in the morning with a headache. I didn't think you'd leave the hut in the dark."

"Will you promise me something?"

"No," he replied.

I forged ahead anyway. "Will you find the boy's family and let them know?"

He didn't answer. We drove in silence.

At the airport I slung the maroon backpack, now filthy with Izapan grime, over my shoulder. The dirt blended with the rest of my person. Exiting the car without saying good-bye, I watched Carlos drive away in his high-priced Hummer. On the plane, I settled in a solitary seat so no one had to sit by me. I needed fumigation. Once I reached home, a hot shower dissolved the dirt into the drain until the water ran cold.

Five days later, I had head lice. After scratching my scalp with a comb and yanking my hair for relief from itching, I finally skulked into a pharmacy to buy *Lice-away*. The weekend dragged by with poison on my head under a plastic cap, killing the critters that caused such misery.

Classes continued. Marisa and I ate, slept, and groused at each other, settling into our familiar coexistence. One evening in early December, I arrived home to find a note on the front door.

Guess what?

I entered to see a footprint cut from fuchsia paper taped to the floor, and then another and another, leading to my home office. On a string hung from the ceiling, whirling lazily, was the sign

We're going to China for spring vacation in March.

Searching for Marisa, maker of signs, I caught sight of a business envelope taped to the bottom of my computer screen. When opened it read:

I found a way.

It will take all our Christmas savings,

but this trip IS Christmas.

Inside the envelope, neatly folded, was the tour name and itinerary, ending at Guilin and the orphanage where, eleven years earlier, I had picked up two-year-old Marisa. The cost was double our Christmas savings. We couldn't afford it.

There was a faint rustle behind me, and I turned to find Marisa in the doorway, eyes sparkling, shiny black hair loose against her shoulders. She had a smile big enough to create my favorite dimple, the one I hadn't seen for a long time.

"Can we go?" The real Marisa shone through, the daughter I loved, the one I would stop breathing for.

I returned her enthusiasm. "We'll have to give up two Christmases," I said. "But it will be worth it."

I opened my arms, and she slipped into them to be enveloped in my love.

On Christmas Day we examined our savings account and scavenged the house for lost cash. We had a treasure hunt under furniture, rifled through cushions, and broke piggy banks to see how much we already had for the China trip. We ate hot dogs for dinner and laughed. It was our best Christmas in years.

12.26.2004

"An undersea megathrust earthquake occurred earlier today with an epicenter off the west coast of Sumatra, Indonesia. The subduction triggered a series of devastating tsunamis along the coasts of most landmasses bordering the Indian Ocean. Death toll is currently unknown, but has reached eleven countries, inundating coastal communities with waves up to a hundred feet high . . ."

As the reporter continued speaking, shock swallowed me whole, leaving numbness at the end of my fingers. The Mayan Venus prophecy stood fulfilled. Desperate to talk to the only person who might have answers, I called Hovard at his home. A woman's voice answered—soft, sultry, feminine.

In my official voice, I said, "This is Dr. Howard. May I speak with Dr. Hovard?"

He didn't take long. "Matt?"

"Have you heard?"

"About the tsunami?"

I didn't mince time. "Did you know it was going to happen?"

The silence was long enough to make me wonder if he'd hung up. When he spoke, confusion shaded the words. "How could I possibly know a tsunami was going to hit Indonesia?"

"Did you know about the Venus transit last June?"

"I'm an astronomer, Matt. Of course I knew."

"But you didn't know it's a harbinger of disaster."

A short pause. "You're upset," he said. "Do you want to come over and talk about it?"

"No, Dr. Hovard. I don't want to bother you."

"Call me Michael. Come over and meet my wife."

I had no desire to meet his wife. Then, I changed my mind.

"Thanks. I need answers."

He gave me the address. Marisa stayed home in front of a movie, gobbling forbidden chocolates. I told her I'd be back soon and then fluffed my hair and put on make-up. Stupid, stupid, stupid.

An attractive slender woman with auburn hair answered the door, no doubt Hovard's wife. Of course she'd be beautiful to match her husband. She offered to take my jacket, but I feigned being cold so I could cover my lack of waistline. We sat on white couches, surrounded by pictures of two children in various stages of growing up. Hovard introduced me to his wife, Lisa, and she went to the kitchen. I pushed to the point.

"I was in Izapa last month, for the New Fire Ceremony."

His face paled. "Did they—?"

"Yes, they did. I also learned about the Venus transit." My words tumbled into each other. "The egress last June was visible from Indonesia, the area that was just destroyed."

Hovard's eyes narrowed. "What are you talking about?"

I slowed down. "I assumed you knew the Mayans followed Venus transits across the sun to predict disasters."

"You assumed too much." He leaned his head sideways, expecting clarification.

I plowed over his confusion, not willing to explain. "Was there a Venus transit in 1883?"

He adjusted to my somber mood. "We can search my programs."

His office was masculine, full of dark leathers, deep green upholstery, oak furniture, and bookcases. Colorful pictures on the walls included the Horsehead Nebula and binary stars, visuals for a science fiction fantasy. While he loaded programs, his wife brought a tray of hot drinks and seasonal snacks, artistically arranged and worthy of a magazine cover. She left like a servant . . . or an uninterested wife.

"Venus transit," he pushed buttons, "happened December 6, 1882."

"And the Krakatoa explosion?"

Click, click.

"It started in May of 1883 and blew its top August 26."

"Six to eight months from the egress," I spoke to myself and then included Hovard. "I need to know when the next transit is due and what countries will witness the egress. Do you have that information?"

He bent his fingers to the task. "The next transit," he finally said, "is due June 5 or 6, 2012."

"It's not exact?" *The Mayans were exact.*

A flash of rebuke surfaced. "For your information, a two-day range is pretty impressive."

I let it drop to ask, "And the egress?"

" . . . will be visible from . . ." he pushed a few keys. "The Venus egress when the sun sets will affect the Caribbean, the northwestern part of South America, and North America."

North America? I had entered a horror movie where a whooshing sound strikes terror, similar to a heart that suddenly jumps in fear. Like my heart.

"It's my responsibility to warn everybody." I stood to walk the floor. "What will convince people there could be danger after the egress?" I heard myself rambling into panic. "They won't believe there *is* such a thing as a Venus transit egress." Still pacing, I tried to reign in some thoughts. "The 1882 transit brought Krakatoa . . . the 2004 egress was followed by the Indonesian tsunami . . . the future June transit in 2012 . . ." I searched Hovard's eyes for help. "How can I warn anybody? How can I—"

"Calm down," he said in his announcer's creamy voice. He walked toward me. "This could be a coincidence."

"No," I spit the word out. "There's a pattern." I groaned, bringing my hands to my face, elbows tight against my sides, hiding from facts.

I felt his arms suddenly around me, pulling me close. "Then we'll study the pattern," he said, calm, collected, assured, charming. "Together."

The initial jolt of surprise dissolved into pleasure. It was the most natural thing in the world to lean my forehead on his chest, fists under my chin. Thin gray stripes on his crisp shirt captured my attention, leading me to cool serenity. His hand moved against my back in a gentle, comforting gesture, and I felt his head touch mine. I remained motionless in the luxury, hoping for forever.

Suddenly embarrassed, I pushed away.

"I'm sorry," I said. "I really lost it for a minute. This is getting too real."

He stayed in place, leaning forward. "What's getting too real?"

The air between us carried unspoken messages. I hadn't experienced that kind of communication in twenty-five years, but I still recognized that look in his eyes, the tone of his voice.

Scrambling to cover my discomfort, I said, "The whole 2012 myth with legends of Seven Macaw and One Hunahpu and the Womb of the Great Mother. It's a fairytale for primitive people who are powerless to change anything." *Run, Matt. Get out.* "Thank you for letting me come and vent. Tell your wife she was very gracious."

I exited the house so fast I thought my image might be left like a cartoon cutout on the front door.

That night I lay under cool sheets, reliving the calming effect of Hovard's arms around me.

A long time ago, during graduate school, I had married. Both of us were working on doctorates. Demands and counter-demands deteriorated into who should cook meals, who should clean, and whose thesis had priority. The air between us screeched with stress. As our relationship headed for the exit sign, I vowed I'd never be a wife again. In the future, if anyone treated me badly, I'd have the option to go home. Now, suddenly, my dead hormones were resurrected. But I was still the master and didn't need complications with a married man. Doubt landed with both feet, suggesting the attraction was one-way, my part.

No. I'm not dead yet. I heard the man's rapid heartbeat.

I forced Hovard's face from my mind and grappled instead with images of human sacrifice, designed to buy time for Earth's survival. A quote surfaced from somewhere in my unused memory banks, a line from Umberto Eco in *Foucault's Pendulum*. "I decided to believe, as you might decide to take an aspirin: it can't hurt, and you might get better."

Sacrifice served as aspirin for the Aztecs, desperate to save their world. I didn't know a remedy for giving up the luxury of Dr. Michael Hovard.

01.10.2005

The Indonesian tsunami killed 230,000 people in the second largest earthquake ever recorded on a seismograph, between 9.1 and 9.3. It caused the entire planet to vibrate as much as 1 centimeter and triggered other earthquakes as far away as Alaska.

But soon the world settled into normalcy. I started a new semester, same classes, same responses, different faces.

My office phone blinked red with a message from Hovard.

"Dr. Howard," the masculine voice addressed me, "I'd like to talk to you. Please call at your earliest convenience." A nice lady would answer the call and be honorable. She would admit she felt attracted to him and it was better to stop all contact. I'm not a nice lady, so I chose to ignore him. *Sorry, Hovard, it's not convenient.*

Two days later, he left another message. "Dr. Howard, I have something you'll be interested in." *I can't afford to be interested in anything involved with you.*

A guest speaker from Egypt lectured at the university about the circular zodiac from the ceiling of the Denderah Temple. He insisted the configuration of stars represented the sky 90,000 years ago, proving the Egyptians understood precession of the equinoxes. Markings on the zodiac showed the movement of solstices and equinoxes, and a line moving through the Square of Pegasus had writing on it, which translated to "the Program of Destiny."

"At exactly 90 degrees to that axis," the man said, "another line can be drawn through the tip of the arrow of Sagittarius, which points to Galactic Centre, where the solstice alignment will occur in 2012."

No sane person should stand in front of a bunch of scientists and make wild statements. If he hadn't been a guest from a foreign country, the entire audience might have drifted away, leaving me as his only listener. I'd heard so many outrageous things the last year, nothing sounded impossible. If Sumerians understood precession, the Egyptians probably did too. Ho-hum.

When the lecture finished, I saw Hovard in the crowd coming toward me and I beat a path to the door, bumping people out of the way.

The next day my office phone rang. I saw Hovard's name and let him leave a message. "Matt, please return my call. It's important."

Not important to me.

Another Sumerian class heaved its way through the *Enuma Elish.* I researched the double names of the god Marduk and the planet Nibiru to confirm they were the same entity. So Marduk is a heavenly body. What can I do with that information?

"Matt!" The message sounded especially clipped through my phone. "You've got to call me!"

I erased it.

The end of January found me in my office eating a tuna sandwich, researching minutia for an article I'd agreed to write. A series of seven impatient raps on the door prompted me to say, "All right! All right! It's open."

Hovard marched in and slammed a large book on my desk.

"After you read this," he snarled, "you'll want to talk to me." He stormed to the door and turned. "Maybe I'll return your call, maybe I won't." Before I could close my astonished mouth, he puffed away like a vapor of smoke, leaving me enveloped in my tuna fish odor.

I picked up the book and stared at the title: *Hamlet's Mill, an Essay Investigating the Origins of Human Knowledge and Its Transmission Through Myth*. Obviously not light reading. The copyright, 1969, was followed by several reprint dates, proving that somebody must be buying the thing.

I randomly opened to page 82 where a quick glance showed, " . . . gods are stars." The Izapan monuments flashed into my mind: The Big Dipper was Seven Macaw. One Hunahpu became the sun.

Page 138: "It was not a foreign idea to the ancients that the mills of the gods grind slowly and the result is usually pain."

Carlos had said: "Prepare your people for pain."

Placing the open book on my desk, I read the words on page 145: "The unhinging of the Mill is caused by the shifting of the world axis." *Are they talking about a pole shift?*

Page 146: "Even Hesiod is far from clear about the early struggles and cataclysms; it is enough that in his *Works and Days* he marks a succession of five ages."

Hesiod . . . Greek poet . . . 700 BC. Five World Ages, like the Mayan belief.

Page 236: "A cosmic event of the first order can be easily

overlooked when it hides modestly in a fairy tale."

I'd been teaching the *Enuma Elish* for twenty years as a story about warring gods. *It isn't. It's about . . .*

I slammed the book shut and pushed it to the edge of my desk. Involvement wasn't an option, not with the book or the astronomer who'd thrown it on my desk. Marisa and I were going to China.

Hovard didn't call again.

ELEVEN

The challenge of China is the language. I once took a stab at Mandarin during a Chinese dig in my grad student days, insulting everyone within hearing. I tried to tell an old woman she was nice but effectively called her a bundle of grass. For the rest of the dig, she hobbled out of her way to avoid me. I gave up my version of Mandarin and never tried again. So when Marisa came home from her school library with an 8½ x 11 inch paperback book called *Learning Chinese in Ten Minutes a Day,* I explained the obstacles.

"The language requires not only unfamiliar words, but also tones, which give every word four different meanings."

Marisa brushed aside my concerns. "I'm Chinese. I'll get it."

"You might 'get it,' " I replied, "because you're young, not because you're Chinese." Her eyes narrowed, chin jutting slightly in defiance, so I hurried to add, "But we can help each other and be grateful that interpreters come with the tour." I'm pretty good at backstrokes.

We sat together on the couch, the large-print paperback on our laps, guessing at tonal marks above essential phrases. In the middle of "Where is lavatory? . . . *Nar you cesuo,*" I interrupted our study.

"Marisa," I asked, "why didn't you get a book with tapes?"

She ducked her head, her voice quiet. "Tapes only came with little books, and I . . . thought a big book would be easier for you to read."

Oblivious to her discomfort, I raised my eyebrows in surprise. "Since when do I need big print?"

Twisting her slender fingers around each other, she answered, "I know you can read little print. But . . . we can't . . ."

Dawn rose inside my head with unaccustomed clarity. My wise little daughter was using the book to force us physically together. I stumbled over my tongue in a rush to give support. "Thank you for being so thoughtful." We snuggled in, with the book spread over our laps. As long as we sat together harmoniously for ten minutes a day, I didn't care if we were learning Chinese or Sanskrit.

Weeks vanished as Marisa bubbled around the house spewing Chinese words and pointing to items. "Shoo" for a book. "Dianhua," a telephone. She twirled in the middle of the room, arms outstretched, chanting, "Wo hen gaosheen hui dao jia" *I am glad to have come home.* By the middle of February, her bags were packed. A week later, she reconsidered her choices and started over. The weather would be bitter in Beijing, only cold in Guilin. What does "cold" mean to a girl raised in the Arizona desert? On the first of March she spread her suitcase contents on the floor to check everything again.

"Slip in a good fork," I suggested.

"What for?"

"Trust me," I replied. "It takes practice to use chopsticks."

"Don't they have forks?"

"Forks aren't considered civilized. Besides," I wiggled my fingers in the air, "the Chinese say using chopsticks increases finger dexterity and improves memory."

She thought about it. "They're right," she announced, pulling up to her five foot height. "Forks are disgusting. I am Chinese and will follow the way of my people."

"That's very poetic," I said, lowering my head to hide a grin. "But you might be glad for a fork."

She tossed the hair out of her eyes as she repacked a yellow sweater. "I don't need a fork."

"You will eat those words," I warned, "with your chopsticks."

I packed two quality forks.

SPRING BREAK / 03.12.2005

The day we left, ten bombs demolished four trains during rush hour in Madrid, Spain. Two hundred were killed, fourteen hundred wounded. *If Mother Nature doesn't hurry and finish us off, our fellow man will beat her to it.*

We boarded Northwest Airlines Flight 70 and found our center section assignments. I settled into the aisle seat in deference to my age, weight, and authority. In twenty-four hours we would enter the looking glass into another world. I pulled out two neck cushions for the long flight over the Pacific Ocean. Two hours later, Chinese stewardesses gracefully served dinner along the narrow walkways. Dressed in red silk jackets with knee-length skirts and a blue and white scarf at the neck, their movements created a dance of dignity. The young woman who stopped at our row had arranged her dark hair in an elaborate knot at the back of her neck. Marisa leaned around me to exhibit her new language skill.

"Ni hao," she said to the lovely lady.

The woman repeated the standard greeting, "Ni hao," followed by a spew of alien sounds. Marisa's face plunged into blank shock. She grabbed her favorite phrase, the one saying she was happy to have come home: "Wo hen gaosheen hui dao jia."

The stewardess smiled vacantly, glancing at me for help. With nothing to offer, I weakly shook my head and shrugged. Marisa slowly repeated the words as the stewardess creased her brows in concentration. I had known we were learning the language wrong but never had the courage to shatter Marisa's belief that

Chinese was written in her DNA. As the stewardess served our trays, I watched my daughter crumble in defeat.

"Hen ben," she mumbled. "Hen ben." *Very dumb, very dumb.*

"No, no, no," the stewardess objected. "Not dumb. Eat now. I come back. I hep you."

"Xiexie," Marisa gushed in gratitude.

After the meal, I offered to trade seats with Marisa so the stewardess could teach the melody of Mandarin without bending over me. I realized too late that I would be squashed against a man with a briefcase and a laptop. Fie on the inconvenience of mother love. The man's hair, light brown sprinkled in gray, bristled its way to his collar. He sported the scruffy mustache and beard of an unkempt hippie. His T-shirt, printed with a picture of the galaxy, had an arrow pointing to the words, "You are here." It wasn't the wild hair, shirt, or beard I resented. It was the unwritten flight rule: if you sit by a man, you automatically lose the arm rest. I collapsed into Marisa's seat and bumped his arm.

"Excuse me," I apologized. "Switching seats gracefully takes a gymnast."

"No problem," he replied, his tone nasal. "It looks like your . . . the little girl . . . is learning Chinese."

"She's my daughter," I said to gratify his curiosity. "We're viewing her heritage, starting in Beijing and ending at her old orphanage in Guilin. Where are you headed?"

He was built in angles with a long, pointed nose. His bulging eyes sat close together, their corners slanting down. I stared at his two-tone scraggle of a beard, black at the chin, white along his jaw, probably bleached. Only his hairdresser knew for sure.

He ignored the scrutiny. "I'm going to Beijing to discuss a book my brother and I wrote. The Chinese want to translate their own edition."

I had to be impressed. My textbook on pottery dating still droned on in English. "It must be an exciting subject."

"It won't be a best seller," he stated flatly. "It's a geometry book about fractals."

"Fractals," I repeated thoughtfully. "I've heard the term." There was an awkward moment of silence as he waited for me to remember. Finally, I had to ask, "Would you remind me what it is?"

"It's the mathematics of nature," he explained, delighted to inform me. "Fractals are everywhere, in snowflakes, mold, bacteria colonies, magnetic fields, lightning, ferns, flowers . . . we're surrounded by them." He taught without exhibiting an air of superiority. I liked him, almost appreciating his creative beard.

"I remember now," I said, pleased at my minutia recall. "It's the 'broccoli factor,' where nature is an infinite copy of itself."

He smiled broadly, prompting me to think his parents should have put him in braces to fix the gap between his front teeth. While I assessed his defects, he praised me. "I like the analogy. We should title the book *The Broccoli Factor*."

I felt guilt for noticing the flaws of a nice guy. "I'm glad I could donate a name to the theory."

His smile did a fast fade to black. I have that effect on people. "It isn't a theory," he sternly corrected.

"Math isn't my specialty," I groveled. "I'd like to hear what you've developed."

He quickly forgave. "Mandelbrot invented it in the 1960s, attempting to measure the coast of Britain. Computers in the 1980s proved him right, complete with a formula." He scribbled an equation on a leftover napkin from lunch: $Z < = > Z^2 + C$. He swiveled the napkin toward me and beamed. "Simplicity is beautiful."

"Very nice," I commented, dashing to a question before the guy launched into a treatise on the formula. "What can you do with fractals?"

"Well, for one thing," he said, grinning, "we can measure the coast of Britain. We can also understand galaxy clusters, or petroleum geology, or the control of fluid dynamics. We make better computers and video games and machines that build copies of themselves. Seismologists determine earthquake distribution, movie makers use fractals for special effects—"

"I'm sold on fractals." I laughed. "But why does China want to publish a translated copy?"

"Because the base of our study originated in China more than four thousand years ago."

I perked up. "Now you're in my field," I told him. "The words 'four thousand years ago' may be the most exciting phrase in the English language." I saw his raised eyebrows and answered his unspoken question. "I'm an archaeologist."

The guy's eyes sparked with something new, maybe respect. He now considered that my dumpy mom image had other facets. "Have you heard of the *I Ching?*" He pronounced it 'Yi Jing.'

"Sure," I said. "Chinese archaeologists excavated a site in 1973 and found an ancient copy of the *I Ching* written on silk, buried in 168 BC. Linguists had the time of their lives comparing the new find with existing translations." I turned to him and confessed, "I picked up an English version at a garage sale. I allow it to sit on my library shelf because it's hardbound in a nice color, but I don't take it seriously. Isn't it just an ancient fortune-telling system?"

"The *I Ching,*" he said testily, "is also called *The Book of Changes.* It's an intricate oracle." Two strikes. I apologized again, and he kept talking. "You toss three coins," he explained, "and count heads as three and tails as two. If the sum is odd, draw a straight line." He created a line on another napkin. "An even number gets a broken line. Do that six times, drawing one above the other, and you get a hexagram." The man sketched a random likeness. "A fortune teller looks up the interpretation, written thousands of years ago by Chinese sorcerers and scholars."

I studied the pattern a few seconds and couldn't resist adding, kindly of course, "In Rome, people used animal livers to tell the future. What's the difference?"

He responded nicely, bless his heart. "Animal livers are messy and not nearly as impressive. The words *I Ching* have three meanings. First: Simple, referring to the universe. Second: Variable, teaching that everything changes. Third: Persistent. Changes follow a pattern that doesn't vary through space or time."

"It's still fortune telling," I asserted.

"It goes much further. Ancient scholars believed time is cyclic in both microcosm and macrocosm. They developed the *I Ching* to determine cosmic patterns."

The discussion was treading uncomfortably close to the Mayan cosmic calendar with its repeating cycles. I shifted, which he mistook for confusion. "In other words," he clarified, "if you know the past, you can tell the future. The *I Ching* measures changes in everything because everything repeats along the same pattern."

"What pattern?"

"The combination of straight and broken lines makes sixty-four hexagrams. We laid them on a computer time-wave scale. It makes a perfect fractal related to any span of time, whether a single day or thousands of years."

This guy made the jaguar tattoo inside my arm itch. He was talking about cyclical time, the kind ancient civilizations used, as opposed to western time which is a straight line going into the future.

I needed his bottom line. "What's your conclusion?"

"In short," he said, "we suspect the *I Ching* is a calendar."

The statement physically jerked me, like a fishing line attached to the inside of my head. "A calendar? How many years does it cover?"

"It's not possible to assign a beginning date to the hexagrams," the bearded wonder affirmed. "Even at a setting of six billion years in the past, the fractal design never varies. Peaks and valleys in the graph provide a history textbook."

I'd gone down the rabbit hole and met the Mad Hatter.

"What historical events could you recognize on a computer time line wave?"

He turned his napkin over to sketch what resembled a metropolitan city skyline with peaked roofs that suddenly plummeted into a chasm at the bottom of the paper before creeping raggedly back to the top and then dipping again—summits and basins, like a stock market graph. "This is the basic model." He pointed with his pen to a dip in the line. "Here you see Nazi Germany. This trough is World War II . . . up here represents the 1960s. Here's the lunar landing resonating to the same pattern as Homeric Greece." I stared at that spot while his pencil skipped to a downward line. "This place, at the 1990s, resonates with the fall of the Roman Empire." He pulled my attention to a lower point. "Here is the murder of students at Tiananmen Square." There was no emotion in his tone. The words moved on a graph of their own, like a picture in a museum. "Saddam Hussein invaded Kuwait at this point, the same place as the birth of Mohammed." I figured the guy was on drugs, but I was stuck in the seat while Marisa practiced pronunciation. My hairy hippie hauled me backwards on the graph. "Here's the American and French Revolutions, this point is the discovery of the New World, and here, in 1356, is the Black Death."

A question exploded in my head. I fought against letting it out, but lost the battle. "How far into the future have you gone?"

"That's the most intriguing part." He drew a circle around the end of the graph line that bumped along the bottom of the napkin. "From 1945, the fractals start to compress. Four thousand years of history are squeezing into sixty-seven years."

It sounded serious. I wanted to lighten the moment. "That might explain the madness of the world right now."

"And the extremes," he added. He wasn't joking.

I pointed to the jagged, horizontal line that began with 1945. "Do you know why the compression happens here?"

"Not a clue. Just that we've been living in a pressure cooker since 1945. There's nothing like it on the entire time line."

If you add 1945 plus sixty-seven years that brings us to . . . .

The man with the bleached hairy jaw continued. "That's not all. The last three-hundred-eighty-four days will be a constriction of the four thousand years plus the sixty-seven years, and the final six days will condense everything into one singularity." He smiled agreeably. "Sort of like the Big Bang."

"Are you talking about the end of the world?" I spoke with blunt bitterness, aware of my small assignment in humanity's survival.

He fixed his pen to the bottom of the graph and drew a flat line until he reached the end of the paper napkin. "That's how the time line finishes." I could almost hear the beeps of a life support system slumping into a single squeal, announcing death.

A dark foreboding drifted at me like a Halloween fog. "Could you figure out the end date?" I already knew the answer.

"By matching the peaks and troughs with key periods in history," the mathematician explained, "we decided the *I Ching* calendar stops at December 21, 2012."

I'd been hit by an asteroid and had to shake my head back into place. "Are you aware of the Mayan calendar?"

He studied me with a sideways look. "Does it involve animal livers?"

He doesn't know. I opened the way for a new topic, using his words. "Animal livers aren't nearly as impressive. The Mayans interconnected three calendars to give daily, seasonal, and long-term events, which repeat like the *I Ching*. Everything ends on December 21, the winter solstice in 2012."

He shrugged. "They probably got it from the Chinese." He had no interest in the Mayans.

"You're probably right," I said pleasantly. "This has been fascinating. May I keep the evidence?" I picked up the napkin.

"Of course." He smiled. "By the way, my beard color is natural."

TWELVE

My conversation with the mathematician died a natural death, but the information sunk in dismally deep. Marisa and I traded seats again. While she watched a movie, I probed the possibility of two ancient cultures independently developing cosmic calendars that ended on the same day. Recent discoveries suggested the ancient Chinese were master seamen; maybe they'd explored Mesoamerica and made contact with the Olmecs. If so, the two calendars should have something in common besides the end date. But one calculated time in the sky, the other an ethereal wave pattern. I couldn't make sense of it. Eventually, the movie captured my brain.

The female tour guide met us at the Beijing International Airport. She appeared supremely young, perhaps in her early twenties, her black hair bluntly cut at her cheekbones, bangs to her eyebrows. The tiny girl barked commands, smoothed chaos at customs, and had us in a bus headed for a hotel within two hours. Marisa bounced in excitement. "Everyone here looks like me," she bubbled.

Our first Beijing restaurant displayed jars of snakes floating in an unidentified liquid, to be chosen the way westerners pick a lobster, except the snakes were already dead, which seemed more humane. "Eat snake," I whispered to Marisa. "Test your Chinese DNA." She wasn't amused.

We sat at a table for six. Luckily the waiter, a burly man who could have been a Sumo wrestler, spoke enough English to take our orders. Nobody wanted spiny fish or dog. When he came to Marisa, his eyes widened slightly at the sight of a Chinese girl among the foreign devils.

"I am Chinese," she said in Mandarin words the stewardess had perfected for her. "I eat with chopsticks."

"Very good, little sister," he replied in English. Marisa beamed.

The waiter brought tin forks for the table and a long, paper-wrapped package for Marisa. The corners of her mouth curved up as she carefully peeled off the thin covering, rolling out two white sticks, smaller at one end. As she attempted to align the sticks between her fingers, one dropped on the table and rolled to the floor. I knew from previous blunders in China that dropping chopsticks is a sign of bad luck. The diners at the next table looked away, embarrassed. Marisa, adding insult, stuck the remaining chopstick in her rice bowl to keep it stable while she bent to retrieve its fallen comrade. Embedding chopsticks in a bowl of rice symbolizes very bad luck. The waiter moved to her side, whisking the offending chopstick from the rice bowl and the other from her fingers as he presented her with a tin fork, two tines slightly bent. I concentrated on my own plate, stabbing a dumpling with my personal stainless-steel utensil. When no one was looking, I slipped a second sturdy fork to Marisa. She accepted gratefully.

The next morning we visited the largest public plaza in the world—the ninety-eight-acre Tiananmen Square, designed to hold a million people. Marisa, bored with venders, noted a long line at the Mausoleum of Mao tse Tung and figured something of interest was happening there. We joined the line. A guard distributed plastic flowers to be placed around the casket. Our little white and purple bouquets were caked with grime. Later, the phony posies could be gathered and used again. Very practical. We shuffled with the crowd through the main entrance of a massive columned building. At the far end of the large room, the embalmed body of Mao lay in a crystal coffin which, we are told, gets lowered each evening into a refrigerated room underneath.

The reverence of the atmosphere prompted Marisa to speak softly. "Why is he so important?"

"He changed the Chinese government," I whispered back.

"Did everybody vote for him to change everything?"

"Nobody voted. He killed thirty million people during his revolution."

"That many soldiers?"

"That many Chinese citizens."

She considered the words and then said, "Well, they seem to like him now."

I'd brought Marisa here to find pride in her birthright, knowing she would never find her mother. Later there would be time enough to explain the Communist Revolution, the Gang of Four, the Red Guard, and the destruction of China's ancient culture. We handed our phony flowers to a guard and walked past the body on display. I felt sorry for Chairman Mao. He had specifically requested cremation.

At the north end of the square stood the entrance to the Forbidden City, the palace of Chinese Emperors, two hundred acres surrounded by a high wall and a moat. If we walked straight through the main buildings, it would take two hours to reach the opposite end of the city. I longed to explore the side streets with their eight hundred yellow-roofed houses—once shelters for officials and their families. Then there were the servant's quarters, and places for the royal guards and concubines. And, of course, the gardens.

Instead, I listened to our guide's memorized script on the composition of doors and pillars. She held her lavender sign higher.

"This way, please." She directed her voice at me as I snooped behind a throne. "We cannot to lose you. Save question for bus."

We passed the Guardian Lions, counted roof charms, and exclaimed over embroidered robes under glass. The main plaza had a river flowing through it, crossed by five bridges. Marisa stood like a carved post, her face mirroring the grandeur.

"If I had stayed in China," she said, staring at the scene, "I would have lived here."

"Nobody," I said without mercy, "has lived here since 1949." Some bubbles, like pimples, have to be popped.

Her response was immediate. "If I'd been born before that, I'd have lived here."

"Sweetheart, if you'd been caught inside these walls, they'd have killed you on the spot. That's why it's called *forbidden*."

She looked across the bewildering expanse of white stone, every column elaborately sculpted, elegant bridges arching the river. She spoke with resolution, head held high. "I would have lived here."

I yielded to her fantasy, throwing facts to the wind. "In another time and place, you might have lived here." She softened, a slight smile creasing the corners of her mouth, like an oriental Mona Lisa.

The next day, the bus took us north to the Great Wall of China, which snaked its way through five thousand miles of rugged mountains in an effort to keep out the barbaric Huns. Marisa and I slipped away from the tour group so she could climb a nearly perpendicular staircase open to tourists. I remained at the bottom to cheer her on, dropping a coin into the slot of a telescope to witness the ascent. She grasped an iron bar to pull herself up the stairs, her long, straight black hair shimmering in the sun. Her yellow sweater, the color of ancient royalty, made her easy to spot.

Two men closed in on her.

My body's entire supply of adrenalin coursed through my legs. I ran like an Olympic sprinter, leaping onto the third step, grabbing the bar to haul myself up. Shrieking Marisa's name, I straddled the pole to help me move quicker, hand over hand, feet pushing at each step like a vertical crab. In the deepest awareness of my mind, I knew the spectacle I presented, but it caught Marisa's attention. She said something to the men and slowly climbed down toward me. With my energy depleted, my forehead dropped, denting itself against the bar. I didn't have enough strength to dismount.

"Mom." Marisa's voice was low in my ear. "You look silly."

Using my last stomach muscle, I lifted my left leg from the bar, clinging to Marisa as we crumpled to the step. I panted like an old, asthmatic dog, except my tongue stayed in my mouth.

"What did . . . those men say . . . to you?"

"They were nice. They said when we got to the top, they'd show me a place nobody knows about." She searched the top stairs. "You scared them off."

"What did I tell you about strangers?"

"They weren't strange. They said in Mandarin that I was pretty, and I understood them. Can I go back up?"

My breathing, still irregular, was strong enough to sputter, "You don't go anyplace without me from now on." I glared intently into her dark eyes. "Do you understand that?"

Marisa leaned away from me, her face rigid. "I'm old enough—"

"No," I cut in. "I'm going to make this direct and candid. In Oriental countries, there's a business that sells children."

Her voice hardened. "Like the one that sold me to you?"

Easy, Matt. This is too important to get deflected. "Remember in grade school when you learned the facts about sex?"

"Yes?" Her tone inflected a question, knowing there was more coming.

"There's a business whose customers pay to use children for sex."

Marisa's eyes creased to slits, reflecting revulsion. "Why would the customer want to do that?"

"They're not normal people. Something is very wrong inside their heads. But they pay a lot of money."

"Then, the children get rich, don't they?"

"The children are slaves, Marisa. The owners get rich."

She stammered her next words. "Why don't . . . can't the parents . . . rescue their children?"

"The business spreads to other countries. Chinese children might be sold into Thailand or Cambodia." I hesitated to complete the horrid picture but decided Marisa should know. "The hardest part is not all children are kidnapped. Sometimes parents sell them."

Her eyes widened. She may have absorbed the words, but I doubted she comprehended their meaning. I'd gone too far and chose to drop the topic. Using the bar, I hauled myself upright, groaning. "It's time to get back to our group." Marisa touched my elbow, pretending to help me down the steep incline. "Tonight," I said, as if child sex slavery had never been discussed, "we'll take the overnight train to Xian, where thousands of life-size clay soldiers once guarded the tomb of the first Chinese Emperor."

Marisa followed my lead in the new direction. "Do we sleep on the train?"

"Beds pull down from the walls. The train rocks us like a cradle."

On the train moving west to Xian, we watched a panorama of China rush past the windows. That night, tucked into my berth of our petite but private stateroom, I realized the music of the rails could either lull one into sleep or into madness. Clack-CLACK, pause, Clack-CLACK, pause.

Marisa's quiet voice drifted up between the bunks. "Why don't the governments do something?"

"About what?"

"About the children."

I allowed a few beats of the train wheels to go by before saying, "They pass laws, but the business pays a lot of taxes, so the law doesn't get enforced."

The silence sounded louder than the track rhythm.

"I guess," Marisa said, "I'm lucky somebody took me to the orphanage."

"Actually, Marisa, I'm the lucky one."

Clack-CLACK, pause. Clack-CLACK, pause. Clack-CLACK, pause.

I hobbled the first day in Xian while my muscles returned to their accustomed indolence. Marisa tried to count the terra cotta soldiers and was thrilled to see that horses were also included. We climbed the stairs on the hill covering the tomb of Qin Shi Huang. As we rested at the top, Marisa asked questions about these earliest ancestors.

"Why did he make an army to protect him after he died?"

"Because he could," I shrugged. "It's nice to be emperor. Fortunately, he accepted soldiers made of clay. Some rulers killed real people."

She moved into deep thought before saying, "That's silly. If I'd been here, I wouldn't have allowed it."

We visited a village school and helped a farmer make soy milk. The people were hard country folk with leather skin and missing teeth. Many of the older men had large facial moles and a few had long hairs growing out of their cheeks. The elderly women doubled over on themselves, their back humps looking like burdens carried under their coats. "If I lived here," Marisa said, "maybe they'd be my grandparents."

I tried to sound nice when I repeated, "Maybe," and hurried her to rent bikes for a ride on the Xian city wall. In the evening we experienced Chinese opera with its orchestra music made from a variety of "boings," like the sound track of a Bugs Bunny cartoon.

In the morning we flew three hours south to Guilin.

Marisa fidgeted, excited and nervous. "Guilin is where you found me."

"At the orphanage."

"My real mother might still be there."

"Maybe." *Not a chance.*

"When can we search for her?"

"We stay with the tour today. Tomorrow, when they see the city, we'll find your . . ." *Not mother, not family, not home,* " . . . orphanage."

We settled in the hotel before boarding a tourist bus. Marisa's nose imprinted itself on the window as we drove past tea plantations, terraced rice paddies, and quaint villages. Our destination was a cruise along the Li River with its famous sculpted mountains, as if a giant child's hand had piled miles of dirt into 300-foot columns and, in a fit of whimsy, shaped them all with round tops.

Marisa's almond eyes were wide with delight. "It's real-life Hobbit country," she exclaimed. Then she added the inevitable words, "If I'd stayed in China, I would have lived here."

Gag.

The boat, not strictly for tourists, was shared with other passengers. Inside the cabin, crude eaters slurped, burped, and farted through their meal. Then they lit up cigarettes, forcing us outside to stand on the boat's deck, wrapping ourselves against the cold as the fantasy mountain ranges faded in the distant mist. Fishermen in colorless coats kneeled on rafts to send cormorant birds into the water as they disgorged captured fish onto flat planks. Bands on the birds' necks prevented them from swallowing until the man had enough fish for his family. I knew that the cormorants themselves were never eaten. When they died, they would be buried with honor.

That evening at the Guilin Hotel, I explained to the guide Marisa's need to see the orphanage where I had found her. The young woman's stone face was more than enough to communicate irritation.

"We do not like our guests to leave the tour."

"We need to see the orphanage."

"You do not perhaps understand the danger."

"We'll take a taxi and pay extra for the driver to wait."

The girl's hand waved once at Marisa. "She is Chinese."

How very astute. "We came here so my daughter could see her heritage." Emphasis on *my daughter.*

"Some do not . . ." she searched for the word, " . . . appreciate that you have taken her."

Aha! By "some" the tour guide means herself.

I concentrated on keeping my back hairs down. "I didn't take her," I said gently, sweetly, agreeably. "I adopted her."

I had known from the beginning that the tour director didn't like me, but I'd attributed it to my maverick ways, peeking around corners, opening forbidden doors. Now it became clear she also didn't like me for having Marisa.

The grouchy guide bowed politely, but her eyes were hard as black rocks. "No one in Guilin speaks English."

Marisa eagerly offered her solution. "I can speak Mandarin," she glanced at me, "a little."

"In Guilin," the woman turned a frosty glare at Marisa, "the accent is different from Mandarin. No one will understand you."

I decided to be the adult and announce our decision. "We'll be fine," I said. "Thank you for your concern."

The guide raised her eyebrows until they disappeared under her bangs, shocked at being defied. "We will not expect you on the city tour tomorrow." She turned and floated away as if small wheels were attached to her feet.

The next morning we slept in, giggled over breakfast, and then approached the hotel concierge with our plans. I placed the address of the orphanage in front of him.

"We need a guide to take us here."

He studied the address, looked at Marisa, and spoke to me in tentative tones, "We haff no guide."

"Just to interpret," I explained. "We'll get a taxi to take us."

The poor man's eyebrows bunched together in panic as he repeated, "Solly, we haff no guide." Maybe those were the only English words he knew.

I turned to Marisa. "Ask him if anyone at the hotel speaks English."

She carefully screwed her mouth into the patterns required for Mandarin. The concierge, confused at first, finally understood her dialect. Nodding vigorously and smiling with relief, he reached for a card on the counter, handing it to me.

Dr. Wu Li is having education to read in the I Ching.

Come to learn of your future in the English.

Apparently, Dr. Li rented a third floor room at the hotel to ply his fortune-telling trade among the tourists. "Li" probably wasn't his real name, since "Li" means profit, and I doubted the title "Dr." was accurate. I admired his cunning in realizing the hotel was better than a back alley stall. The guy deserved a nice tip. We went up to the third floor.

The guy wanted real money.

"I cannot to leave," he said, "because of business loss."

"We'll pay you for your time. How much do you usually make in half a day?" *Probably a couple of bucks.*

"I need," I could hear his synapses buzz, "twenty dollar."

"That sounds fair for the day."

"For hour."

I guessed the man as middle-aged. His hair might have been cut using a bowl as a pattern, leaving the thick top to spread in the air. His long face had eyes almost as high as the forehead, which left his nose to make an exclamation point in the middle. The mouth crowded itself under the nose, almost falling off his chin. He sat behind the room desk, surrounded by tattered books and charts. I could cut the guy a break.

"Tell you what," I said, all business, no smile. "I pay you twenty dollars for the day plus *I Ching* fortunes when we come back." I watched expectantly, hoping he'd accept the deal.

"Not enough," he said.

" . . . and," I rapidly added, "we'll tell all the others on our tour about you."

He hesitated. I moved in for the kill. "Not only that, I'll rewrite your advertising in perfect English."

"Okey dokey," Dr. Li said seriously.

By noon we sat in the back seat of a blue and orange taxi traveling north to the Guilin Social Welfare Institute, 1 Fuli Road.

The city of Guilin and its province of Guangxi is legendary, surrounded by the same limestone cliffs that jut from the banks of the Li River.

"Marisa," I leaned over to say, "this is the place you would have been if you had stayed in China."

"It's prettier than Arizona," she said. "Anything is."

I leaned back, rolling my eyes to the ceiling of the cab. After stops, starts, and turnarounds, the taxi pulled to the curb of a long lane stretching to meet a drab brick building. The driver used hand motions to indicate that he wouldn't drive in the lane—too hard to turn around. Dr. Li, Marisa, and I walked in the frigid air, a cold breeze whipping at our reddened cheeks and tousling our hair. We posed for a picture in front of the building as if it were a common tourist site. Dr. Li used my camera to take the photo. As we entered the building, Marisa held tightly to my hand. Our footsteps echoed through the lobby and down the stark hall to the office. Nothing had changed in eleven years, not even the eerie silence. I knocked at the closed door, its opaque glass reinforced with chicken wire.

A woman's voice spoke, and Dr. Li ushered us in. He warbled his Chinese tune, nodded at Marisa, and placed our orphanage paperwork on her desk. She examined the papers, sang a few words, and we followed her to another room. Briskly pawing through files, she pulled one out and set it on a table. Dr. Li conferred and then turned to Marisa.

"You . . . baby . . . put down at Gate 1, close to police. They take you to here. No name with you. No more." The woman picked up the file to return it.

"No, wait." Marisa didn't even try her Chinese, addressing the orphanage worker in English. "Don't you recognize me? Didn't anyone come here for me? Did a lady come asking about me?"

Dr. Li and the woman consulted briefly. "No one ever come for you," Dr. Li translated. "No one come for any children. The lady say . . . she happy to see you have the good life."

The silence that followed made the air around us itchy. This was the dead end I knew Marisa would have to face. We couldn't leave yet.

"Dr. Li," I said, "please ask her if we could see the room where Marisa stayed."

They mumbled a short while and Li said, "She take you for see."

The building where Marisa had lived still remained, sparse and square, with cold concrete walls and floors. Bits and pieces of toys sat on a ledge—a red box, a Caucasian doll with strands of blonde hair.

"Where are the children?" Marisa asked.

Dr. Li supplied the answer. "They prepare for eat."

The straight, narrow hall led past soundless closed doors. We turned a right angle into a large room holding ten tables. At each table, six children of varying ages sat calmly, their lovely round faces turned toward us, smiling. After one frozen moment, Marisa bounded to a table, greeted the children, and introduced herself. I followed her example until we had met every child, touching hands, grinning, giggling, crying a little, and laughing. They chanted a Chinese song for us. We performed "Twinkle, Twinkle, Little Star." When we left the room, waving good-bye, Marisa turned to the *I Ching* reader.

"They were all girls. Can we sing to the boys?"

"Only girl here," he said. "In China are saying: Girl maggot in rice. Goose better than girl." The man spoke the hateful words without a shred of discomfort for what they meant to Marisa. It was just a history lesson. No sons, no happiness.

Marisa stood unmoving in the hallway that had once been her home. "Mom?" I didn't want to hear her question. She had just plummeted from Empress of China to throw-away orphan girl.

"Did my mother give me away because I'm a girl?"

"Of course not," I spoke too quickly. "We don't know who left you at Gate 1. Your mom must have died and a very kind person took you where they knew you'd be safe." Marisa's eyes disappeared behind a haze of tears, and I dashed into their depths to save her.

"They left you here for two years until I could come and get you." My voice pleaded to be heard, cracking with emotion. "Because I'm your mom . . ." I kneeled on the floor before her. "Ni shi wode beibei." *You are my baby.*

"I want to go home," she said, collapsing against my neck, grieving for the loss of what she never had. I wrapped her in my arms, grateful to be the mother of this brave-spirited survivor.

We both wept.

THIRTEEN

Back at the hotel, Dr. Li reminded me of our agreement. He would arrange a trip to the orphanage, we would buy *I Ching* readings and give him a new advertisement in perfect English. I told him he could tell Marisa's fortune while I fixed the errors on his card.

"Two," he said. "I give good deal."

"I'll give you a little extra to do only Marisa's fortune."

"Two," he repeated. "Good deal."

In his third floor office he put his fortune-telling equipment on the desk: three coins and a long sheaf of brown papers, hand bound between two boards, cracked with age. His father and grandfather had probably used it. Marisa asked me to go first so she could see how it was done.

"What is question?" The man folded his hands on the desk, long fingers intertwined. I took too long, and he motioned one hand impatiently, as if waving away a mosquito.

"Go, go," he said.

All right, all right. "How can I . . . uh . . . do my current project?"

I threw the three coins, he counted the sum and then drew a straight line. The next three tosses were all broken lines, drawn above the first. The fifth throw had a sum that equaled "straight" and the sixth produced a broken line to finish the hexagram.

Li consulted his brown papers, flipping through the sixty-four patterns until he found the hexagram matching mine and began the reading.

"This name 'Chun' mean difficult beginning." *No kidding.* He intoned from the *I Ching* oracle. "Do not push too hard, but do not to give up. Help of Sage important."

A Sage?

Li's finger moved up the hexagram. "Broken in number two place mean solution come, but obligation come also. Not good. Wait for good solution."

What obligation? What solution?

Dr. Li explained the third line. "Bad feeling make you want give up work. Do not to do. Bring misfortune."

He continued translating the fourth line from his brown, crumbling papers. "Four place say: Dark will hide light. Go slow. Have method. Quiet balance."

The fifth line warned: "Do not act alone. Seek advice of Sage. Be patient until path is clear."

Who is this Sage?

Li moved to the top. "Unite if sincere. Sage will bring good fortune."

The little man stared into my eyes until I squirmed. "Who are you?" he asked.

I answered truthfully. "I'm nobody."

"You have great duty. Must have help, is no disgrace."

The man leaned into a cardboard box on the floor, his black

hair bobbling on his head. He rose again with a thin, gray paper and handed it to me. It contained my *I Ching* fortune in English. The guy could have given it to me at the beginning and saved time, but he couldn't have charged as much money.

I glanced at the handwritten paper. "The *I Ching* tells me to find a sage," I said. "Does it say where to find one?"

The little Chinese man raised both eyebrows. "You know already."

I was afraid of that.

FOURTEEN

04.01.2005 / SCOTTSDALE, ARIZONA

Hovard was my sage. I had angered him by ignoring his efforts to reach me. The damage had to be repaired. *Hamlet's Mill* supplied an excuse, but I wouldn't be able to read the encyclopedic essay casually. It had to be slogged through. For a long, miserable week I studied the book, drudging through pages like the mill of the gods grinding its slow course across the sky.

I called the astronomer and left a no-pressure message. "Dr. Hovard, this is Dr. Howard. I'm reading your book. Thanks for loaning it to me."

No response. No surprise.

At least I could take the two creators of *Hamlet's Mill* seriously. Both had earned degrees from the University of Frankfurt and both were current MIT professors. They'd collected every ancient legend in the world about mills of the gods crushing out disasters; axles falling from their frames in the sky; the tree of life spreading into the Milky Way. From Finland to Egypt, Iceland to Iran, India, Polynesia, Greece, China—each culture told cosmic stories interpreted by precession of the equinoxes.

I left another message. "Dr. Hovard, your book is intriguing. I'd like to discuss it with you."

I got the silent treatment—well deserved.

The authors of *Hamlet's Mill* threw barbs at their fellow scientists for allowing biological evolution to deny human intelligence. Page 69: "The lazy word 'evolution' has blinded us to the real complexities of the past." Page 71: "Mistaking cultural history for a process of gradual evolution, we have deprived ourselves of every reasonable insight into the nature of culture."

I left another message for Hovard. "This is Dr. Howard," *who is trying not to sound desperate.* "Please return my call."

He'd probably looked at my name and erased the message as I spoke. I hated to face him in person without knowing his attitude toward me. A phone conversation could save some groveling.

Two days later, I made another attempt. "Hey, I've just learned that the four corners of the world are really the equinoxes and solstices. This book is brilliant." *That ought to get him.*

It didn't.

Eventually, inevitably, I entered the astronomy building, walked past Foucault's Pendulum, and knocked on Hovard's door.

"Come," he called.

The door opened to make a frame around me. I had *Hamlet's Mill* clutched to my heart. "Basic astronomy," I solemnly announced, "should be required for archaeologists."

I waited for him to say, "Then take a class" or "That's not my problem" or "Close the door on your way out." Instead he questioned curiously, "Did you actually read it?"

Considering the fact I didn't understand it, I said, "I saw every word."

He caught the joke and broke into laughter. "Sit down and tell me what you think."

Relieved, I asked, "In twenty-five words or less?"

"That would be remarkable."

I settled into the chair across from him, preparing for the challenge and raising one finger to designate the first point. "Prehistoric people had our brain capacity . . . maybe more, since they understood precession without computers." A second finger punctuated the next thought. "Cosmic realities were told in fairy tales. Their gods were stars." I leaned back into the chair. "Did I make it in twenty-five?"

He reviewed the words. "Twenty-four, actually."

"Then I deserve another twenty-five."

He spread his arms in agreement.

"Our modern arrogance," I began, "keeps us from admitting that ancient people had knowledge, which prevents us from understanding our own history. It's a crime against science." I settled into the chair, satisfied.

Hovard's groomed salt and pepper goatee curved in a grin. "You've condensed four hundred pages into less than fifty words. That's astounding."

"Get over it. I'm going to start asking questions and I expect answers."

The mustache turned down. "I had answers last month, but you didn't seem interested."

Lie, Matt. Make it good. "I apologize for not calling right away. I took my daughter to China." *A half truth.*

He considered the excuse for a count of three seconds and then shifted in his chair. "Ask," he said.

"I need an analysis of the *Enuma Elish.* I don't think it's about gods. I think it teaches astronomy. To begin, the gods are disorganized, warring against the water dragon, Tiamat. Can you translate that?"

He answered pensively. "The Solar System was chaotic. A large water world kept the other planets from stable orbits."

I carried on with the story. "Marduk, alias the star Nibiru, approaches the gods to get weapons so he can attack Tiamat."

"My guess," Hovard offered, "is that a rogue planet was captured by the gravitational pull of the outer planets. As it moved through our universe, it picked up satellites, even moons."

My turn again. "In the Sumerian tablets, the battle gets grisly. Marduk uses his weapons to strike Tiamat's heart and gut her belly with lightning and fire. He leaves the dead goddess, returning later to decide what to do with the carcass. He cuts her in half, scattering the lower part across the heavens. The 'head' became Earth."

Hovard nodded, a sign he understood the scene. "Marduk came so close to Tiamat that his satellites hit the water world. The lightning and fire could have been electromagnetic charges between the two giants. Marduk returned to its orbit, which now included our solar system. On the next flyby, he cut the planet Tiamat in half, forming the Asteroid Belt between Mars and Jupiter, and knocking the other half into the third path to become Earth."

I moved to a condensed ending. "Marduk becomes ruler of the universe. He organizes the gods with 'tablets of destiny' and creates humans. After that, the epic says he crossed the heavens and surveyed its regions. One of his names is 'god of the crossing.' "

Hovard thought a minute. "Marduk's entry into the solar system destroyed the huge water world and pushed planets into gravitationally sound orbits. The 'tablets of destiny' might refer to the paths around the sun. When the upper half of Tiamat moved to the third orbit, sulphurous volcanoes paved the way for life. As 'god of the crossing,' Marduk became part of our solar system."

We stared at each other until I looked away. "I need astronomy facts to back all that."

The man settled into his chair as if he had a lot to say. "During the last part of the 1700s, scientists noted that planets were spaced according to a mathematical formula. But the asteroid belt spoiled the picture by floating in the fifth orbit. In 1802 a German astronomer, Heinrich Olbers, first suggested the belt was a destroyed planet."

"So the asteroid belt is part of Tiamat?"

"Possibly. Other scientists said there wasn't enough mass to account for a planet."

Obnoxious with enthusiasm, I hooted in delight. "The *Enuma Elish* explains it! Half of Tiamat became Earth. So the third rock from the sun . . . us . . . used to be the fifth rock, Tiamat, which collided with Nibiru."

Hovard smiled indulgently. "Several astronomers have favored the theory, never realizing the Sumerians wrote it first. Hartman is one, Alvarez another. In 1993, Van Flandern wrote a book on it. In 2003 a French astronomer, Morbidelli, asserted in *Science* that the solar system was originally chaotic. A collision rearranged it."

My eagerness bordered on adolescence. "Done by Marduk, also known as Nibiru."

Hovard nodded. "And Marduk may be returning."

The fun part was over. I forced myself to become a serious adult. "Explain," I commanded.

"In 1982," he began, "NASA issued a press release stating they'd discovered a large mystery object beyond the outermost planets."

"I remember the headlines," I said. "The press called it Planet X."

"*The Washington Post, U.S. News*, and *Newsweek* reported it. Then NASA withdrew their announcement, claiming it was a mistake."

"Because . . . ?"

"They know something's coming," Hovard casually stated, "but don't want the masses to panic. There's a definite climate change happening. Politicians blame household sprays and fossil fuels, but glaciers and ice caps are not thawing on the surface, they're melting underneath the ice. Electromagnetic forces are affecting the sun, which is impacting our core."

"Could that generate a pole shift?

He nodded. "Which could cause the loosened ice caps to slide into the ocean, triggering tidal waves over entire continents."

"So you're saying Planet X is responsible for crazy weather and a possible polar shift."

"I'm saying something big out there might be pushing at us."

"Why can't we see it?"

"It's below us. NASA is observing whatever it is from the South Pole."

His words wrapped around me, restricting my breathing. "Do I dare ask when this thing is coming?"

"Since it doesn't officially exist, we're not getting updates."

"So, Planet X is an unknown quantity. Give me the bad news."

"If it shoves us into a pole shift, two thirds of Earth's population will perish. Superstorms with 300 mile per hour winds could rage across the planet while mega tsunamis inundate every coast. After that, two thirds of survivors would die of famine and exposure in six months."

Famine. The word sounded foreign. In this country, food supplies are beamed into grocery stores like dispenser machines on the starship *Enterprise*. Starvation is impossible. I sat still, grimly rounding my arms around Hovard's book.

He directed my thoughts. "What are the essentials for survival?"

Memorized words surfaced from my Girl Scout days. "Food, water, shelter."

"Start there. People don't need *Hamlet's Mill.*"

Hovard's words reminded me that his book still leaned against my chest. I placed it on the desk in front of him. "You know what's missing in this book?" My finger jabbed at the cover. "There's no hypothesis. They've collected proof of ancient precession knowledge without answering 'why'? *Why* did early people care about a clock in the sky with a 26,000-year little hand? Why did they create legends for uneducated people to pass on?"

Hovard leaned toward me. "You're the one with the mark. You'd better know the answer."

"I don't want the mark," I snapped. "I'm an ordinary teacher in the wrong place and time, getting an impossible assignment that should have been yours." I glared at him. "You're the sage who knows it all."

He ignored my poison, quietly offering support. "I didn't know about the underground government preparations. I'd never heard of the Venus egress warning. Are there other things you haven't told me?"

A heavy net of weariness dropped over me. "Did I mention the Chinese *I Ching* is a cyclical calendar that ends in 2012?"

Surprise transformed his face. "Where did you hear that?"

"On the plane going to China. The guy had written a book."

Rebuke carried his words. "Are you deaf *and* blind? These things find *you*, not me. There are no mist—"

"Don't." I pushed from the edge of his desk, stood, and walked toward the door.

"Before you go . . ." his tranquil voice stroked the back of my neck. I turned to see him with one elbow on the arm of his chair, chin resting on his fist. " . . . propose your hypothesis for *why*."

Drained, I propped myself against the wall. "Ancient people from previous ages are trying to warn us of what's coming. They saw it, lived through it, and sent myths and legends into the future. It's not just the end of an age but the end of the great cycle. There might even be a planet on its regular orbit that could cause a pole shift . . ." I closed my eyes, " . . . unless the black hole at the center of the universe eats us first."

When I opened my eyes, Hovard had changed position, arms on the desk. "You should understand by now that 2012 isn't the end. It's the beginning."

"Yeah, yeah, yeah, I know." I spoke the words singsong, like memorized lines. "We're in a seventy-two year time period, with 2012 at the center. It's like a new birth, squeezing events into a singularity until survivors find themselves on the other side."

Hovard nodded and picked up where I'd left off. "There's also a mysterious time designation that the Mayans called 'a Time of No Time' that lasts twenty years. It's an intense transition between ages when the galaxy's center releases a burst of light. It happens every 5,125 years, like the beating pulse of the universe."

"And what ghastly thing happens then?"

"I don't know."

In words weighted with cynicism, I said, "Twenty years or seventy-two years or both combined, it doesn't matter. If only a couple of your disasters happen, nobody will survive."

"They might." He waited for me to defuse. "People need to prepare with food, water, and shelter."

"Do you really think anybody will listen to that drivel?"

"Probably not, Matt, but they deserve a chance."

In a sudden, unexpected detour, I asked, "How long have you been calling me 'Matt'?"

He adjusted to the new topic. "I guess always."

"You're 'Dr. Hovard' to me." I pushed myself from the wall. "I asked you to use 'Michael.' "

"Yes, I remember. At your home, when I met your wife."

He bowed his head slightly and then raised it. "We should probably discuss that event. I apologize for crossing professional boundaries, but I admit I felt something. I think you did too." He waited for me to agree, but I stood silent. He continued. "I married for beauty when I was too young to understand the importance of companionship. She reads fashion magazines and takes quizzes titled *Is There Romance in Your Marriage?* I want to discuss deep subjects with someone who understands me. It gets lonely at my house."

"If you'd married for brains," I chided him, "you'd trade it for beauty."

His reply was wistful. "Probably. Too bad the combination is so rare."

A spot in my head twanged, like a guitar string snapping. *You juvenile jerk. You selfish slime.*

I opened the door. "You've given me something to think about, Dr. Hovard. I should let it settle."

The door made a soft click behind me.

FIFTEEN

On the walk across campus, my thoughts tumbled into anarchy, refusing to obey my will. *Mayan witch doctors in Sumerian texts and fairy tales; Venus transits guided by murdered teenagers; end of the world legends told by hypnotic astronomers . . .* Gradually, a soft rhythm emerged as the words of Lewis Carroll's "The Walrus and the Carpenter" entered the chaos.

> "The time has come," the Walrus said,
> "To talk of many things:
> Of shoes—and ships—and sealing wax,
> Of cabbages—and kings—
> And why the sea is boiling hot—
> And whether pigs have wings."

If Hovard was the sage, I was the pig with wings. It was time to fly away. I'd been living in one of those nightmares that feels absolutely real while you're in it.

When I entered my office, the potted plants, books, file cabinets, and overstuffed chair in the corner shook me awake. My framed pictures of Dvaraka, the sunken city off the coast of India, came into focus for the first time in several months.

I noticed color in the poster of Tiahuanaco—the enigmatic Bolivian ruins. Sitting in my swivel chair, I stared at the candy dish on my desk, wondering where it had been all year. I considered the courageous cactus on the desktop, placed there because a Swiss researcher said a cactus could absorb electromagnetic pollution from computer screens. The ugly plant survived whether I loved it or not, an example I could follow. I touched its spines, pricking my finger, and then watched a drop of blood ooze into existence until it splattered on my transparent desk pad. The red splotch shouted the reality of my life, the one I still had. Dead Mayans and their traditions had no power over me. Neither did living sages and their Barbie Doll hang-ups.

Giddy, I rocked back and forth in my chair for a minute as I examined the article I'd been writing. It was terrible, deserving of death. I cheerfully tossed it in the trash and started over, my fingers probing the keyboard, laying brilliant prose on the screen. Thirty minutes of effort produced the article's introduction.

I spoke to myself. "The Old One made the mistake. He'll have to fix it. I'm taking back my life." The jaguar inside my arm might even be an advantage, giving me a mystique of my own. How many professors have a tattoo?

"I'm out," I announced to the ceiling. "Welcome home, Matt."

The month of April skipped euphorically to the end of the semester in May. I ate large, robust meals and went to movies with Marisa. My article virtually wrote itself, except for a minor point that could be cleared by someone in the geology department. I decided to walk over, an excuse to get out and enjoy the perfect weather that matched my current life. With a breeze in my face and sunshine on my shoulders, my feet barely touched the ground, a prelude to the coming plunge.

The geology department, which studies things older than dust, had a very young secretary.

I began the tedious introduction. "I'm Dr. Howard from archaeology. Can someone answer a question about dating stone tools with thermoluminescence?"

The secretary offered to check. I scanned the office. On a bulletin board, an 8 x 10 inch map of the American mainland seemed skewed. Closer inspection showed a pen and ink drawing with broken lines designating the states. One dark, jagged boundary had sliced off California, half of Washington, and—

"Dr. Spokes will see you."

She ushered me into his office, and he invited me to sit.

"You've got a strange U.S. map out there," I blurted. "Where did it come from?"

He smiled. "One of our graduate students designed it as part of his master's degree. It's a futuristic vision of disaster, based on geologic data. We have permission to make copies if you want one."

"Thank you. I'd also like to read the thesis."

"It's not published, but I can give you the boy's contact information."

He escorted me back to the secretary, giving her instructions. Soon I held my own copy of the map along with the number of a student named Kaha'i Boyd.

Between the geology and archaeology departments, I leaned against a tree to study the geology map of destruction. The nightmare I thought I'd escaped had just yanked me back to its solid existence. Dazed, I returned to my office.

Impatiently, I pushed a stack of papers from my desk to the floor, slamming the map on the cleared place. Pulling a current U.S. map from the files, I compared it to the boy's creation.

It looked like the hand of a misshapen water monster had grabbed America from beneath. One palm covered most of Nevada, half of Utah, and a third of Arizona, its fingers touching Idaho. I spent time analyzing Arizona, wondering how the map would affect Marisa. It looked like our house might end up as beachfront property, with too high a price.

My eyes moved to the monster's elongated fingers, which had

submerged the western half of Washington and Oregon. There was no California. The ogre's other hand had lifted itself from the Gulf of Mexico to squash from existence Louisiana, Arkansas, Oklahoma, Missouri, and most of Illinois. Only the western half of Kansas and Texas remained with a little sliver of Oklahoma in the middle.

The map was a visual aid for Hovard's words at our first interview: "There aren't enough sand bags in the world to hold back the Gulf of Mexico when it comes up the Mississippi."

At the top of the map, Lake Michigan disappeared under the beast's fourth finger, along with half the state of Michigan. The East Coast lost all its beautiful, small states. Florida was gone.

I called the boy's number. A deep, rumbling voice answered.

"Yo. It's me."

"Uh . . . is this Kaha'i?"

"Hey, Icky," he yelled away from the mouthpiece. "This one's for you. It's female." He uttered a nasty laugh.

A higher-pitched voice spoke into the phone. "Hello?" He sounded expectant, probably hoping I'd really be a girl. I hated to disappoint him.

"I'm Dr. Howard from the archaeology department. You designed an unusual map of the United States. I need to talk to you about your work. Could you come to my office as soon as possible?" I pulled rank, not wanting him to slip away.

"Yeah, sure," the kid spoke nervously. "When?"

"Now."

SIXTEEN

Kaha'i Boyd sat across from my desk, hunched like a mouse caught in a trap. The deep brown hair on his forehead was shaggy, nearly obscuring his dark, apprehensive eyes. His shoulders were stooped, forcing his head and neck forward like a beaten buzzard.

"Am I in trouble?" His worried eyebrows nearly slid off the sides of his temples.

"Why would you think that?"

"My thesis committee . . ." The boy timidly shrugged. "They didn't like my topic. They said it came close to science fiction and would offend scholars." He produced an uneasy laugh. "Since I'm at the top of my class, they let it pass."

"Top of the class, huh?"

He turned his head to stare at the wall. "I'm a geek."

I took pity on the slouching boy. "Geeks rule the world, you know."

"Not my world." A touch of bitterness edged his tone. I'd already had a taste of his roommate.

I tried to comfort him. "Your committee wouldn't approve your master's thesis without convincing evidence."

He shrugged as an answer.

"Where are you from?"

"Hawaii."

I went along with his short response. "You left Hawaii for the desert?"

"Scholarship," he said, sinking lower in the chair. "I accepted this one so I'd be forced to study." His attitude whispered apology.

"Couldn't you study in Hawaii?"

"Desert's better. Nothing else to do."

I'd keep getting short answers unless I earned a little trust. "I owe you an explanation for my interest in this." *Not the truth, of course.* "I'm researching ancient disasters to explain some puzzling archaeology. I'd like to know more about your thesis." I pushed the map in front of him. He stared at it as if he'd never seen it before and I bumbled ahead. "For example, where does all the water come from that could cover this much land?"

The geology student roused from his stupor. "Centrifugal force makes sea level at the equator four hundred feet higher than any place else. If the rotation of Earth changes, the water will slosh over every coastline in the world."

"Why would the rotation change?"

His shoulders did their up and down motion as he said uncertainly, "Maybe a pole shift?"

I leaned toward him, forearms on the desk, an invitation for him to enlighten me.

He took the hint. "There are two kinds: magnetic and crustal. Magnetic pole shifts happen all the time . . . geologically speaking. Scientists can count at least 181 events when the magnetic field of Earth collapsed and re-established itself at the opposite pole, so north is south and vice versa."

"And the result?"

"Nothing huge." I encouraged more information with the arch of an eyebrow. He went on. "If there's a magnetic field collapse and a magnetic flux line change, then the ozone layer sort of disappears."

"Sort of?"

"Not completely, but ozone is an unstable molecule with a

forty-five minute half life. If it got that low, the Benthic layer, would get knocked out, killing a lot of fish and most of the grassy plants on Earth."

"By 'grassy plants' you mean things like wheat and rice?" He nodded once, so I kept going. "What's the Benthic layer?"

"It's where all the nutrients are. Probably kill lots of trees, too."

"That sounds serious to me. You said a magnetic pole shift wasn't a big deal."

"It's minor compared to crustal displacement."

I wondered if he could hear me hold my breath.

"Scientists," the geology student continued, "accept magnetic pole shift, but they don't think a crustal displacement is possible, even though there's evidence."

"I assume that's the second kind of pole shift and the crust physically moves. What's the evidence?"

Fidgeting, Kaha'i entered his no-comfort zone. "Hapgood wrote a book about it in the 1950s. Einstein did the preface. Mather agreed with the theory. But most scientists were getting into plate tectonics and didn't like crustal shifting because it happens too fast." He met my eyes. "Geologically speaking." The boy scratched at the side of his neck and then looked away. "This is the part where I get into trouble."

"I promise not to tell your committee," I reassured him. "Start at the beginning."

"Several thousand years ago—"

"You don't need to go back that far."

The kid's face formed a quarter smile. "I learned in high school that several thousand years ago the North Pole was closer to Wisconsin and the South Pole was in the Indian Ocean. Siberia used to be tropical a short time ago." He stopped.

"Geologically speaking," I added, to let him know I understood.

"Frozen mammoths," he continued, "had foliage in their stomachs and buttercups still in their mouths. They were suffocated while standing and ended up with broken bones, sunk in permafrost, intact."

"That sounds like a quick freeze."

"Right," Kaha'i affirmed. "I started questioning the speed of geologic changes. An ice age apparently fell right on top of the mammoths in Siberia. In Antarctica, ice core analysis shows the continent was once ice-free, while North America was buried in the stuff. This led me to wonder about rapid crustal displacement."

"How rapid?"

He returned to the shrug. "Weeks, maybe days. For mammoths, the change had to be instant, at least a minus hundred degrees Celsius to freeze them that fast."

"That's way beyond scientific thinking," I blurted. The kid was delusional.

"I've learned to keep quiet," he explained. Then suddenly he perked up. "But I have a hero now. He's a Princeton geologist, Adam McIff. He examined ancient rocks in Norway and found proof of crustal pole shifts in magnetic minerals. The North Pole has shifted more than 50 degrees in less than 20 million years." Kaha'i gave a Cheshire Cat grin, impish, full of mischief. "Nobody questions McIff's research. He's planning to look for more evidence in Australia. I think he'll find it."

"How big is a fifty-degree change?"

"The distance from the equator to Alaska."

I was astonished and I don't even understand geology. When I took it in college, I cheated to get a passing grade. "Does your hero have theories?"

"He said there could be four causes . . ." Kaha'i Boyd switched to a different language, with words like rapid plate tectonic rotation during depositional hiatus and subducting plates. I watched him visibly transform, straightening his back, tossing the hair out of his eyes when he talked about nongeocentric axial dipole fields. After describing plate harmonic frequencies and piso electric slip threshold, he noticed my glazed eyes.

The genius geek slowed down to pick me up. "Anyway, McIff said his observations are best explained by rapid shifts in paleogeography associated with a pair of true polar wander events."

The terminology made me dizzy. "Is that the second kind of pole shift? Crustal displacement?" I offered him the candy dish on my desk. He took a chocolate Kiss, unwrapped it, and popped it in his mouth. "Yemmph," he said.

"Does that mean 'yes' or 'I like chocolate'?"

"Both," he mumbled enthusiastically. The boy's friendlier alter ego had surfaced. He reached for a second candy.

I posed another question. "When McIff says 'rapid,' does he think a few days, like you, or a few million years?"

"If he thought like me," Kaha'i shook his head, "he'd get kicked out of Princeton."

"Maybe he's learned to keep quiet too."

"Nah, he's legitimate," the student retorted. "But he's made a huge step forward."

Time for a change of subject. "I'd like a closer look at your map. It appears that safe places are primarily in the Midwest."

He shook his head and swallowed the chocolate. "This is the map that only shows flooding. My thesis includes earthquakes, tornados, and volcanoes, according to geologic structure. Did you know 90 percent of volcanoes are under the ocean?" The kid jumped like a frog into the closest puddle of interest, swimming in a tangent over the Ring of Fire in the Pacific Ocean.

I pulled him out of the water. "Let's get back to the map. Show me a safe place."

He spoke bluntly. "The U.S. hasn't got a safe place."

It took a few seconds to recover from the blow. "What are people supposed to do?"

"I'm a geology student, not a sociologist." Kaha'i did the patented shrug. "I suppose if somebody wanted shelter, they could go into the mountains . . . not on top, of course, but in a sheltered valley. People should know there's a downside to West Coast mountains, since they were formed from subduction. If there's a projectile thrust, rocks will fly around like bullets. But the mountains are still better than coasts that might be flooded 200 to 500 miles inland." Kaha'i spoke as if he were discussing dinner instead of death. "Forests are a bad idea because of fires . . . caves can collapse. The salt flats would be stable, but not safe during massively high winds. People could build little concrete hobbit houses because domes are good in wind. But when it's over, they'd starve because nothing grows on salt. The best thing would be an underground shelter, except it could end up burying you alive. Or you could move to the Antarctic which doesn't have plate pressure, or—"

I broke in. "How about Arizona?" *Tell me how safe Marisa is.*

The new Kaha'i Boyd turned eager to talk. "Except for water coming in from the coast, Arizona would stand. The state is built on prehistoric rock bed that won't crumple. But Arizonans need the outside world for everything, and the outside world won't be there anymore. Refugees from the south will overrun the place. A lot of people will fight and kill and starve."

"You're a bundle of laughs, kid. What will *your* home be like?"

"Hawaii is stable. It'll go under, and then surface again."

I wondered if Kaha'i had warned his family and then asked my pivotal question. "When?"

He was perplexed. "Excuse me?"

"When could all this happen?"

He smiled. "My Hawaiian name means 'one who tells' but I'm not a soothsayer." He suddenly lit up and did one of his frog jumps to another swamp. "Do you know Fritz Dressler?"

"Not personally," I tried to keep my balance. "I like his travel photography."

"Dressler said: 'Predicting the future is easy. It's trying to figure out what's going on now that's hard.' That describes me. I know what my future is, I just can't figure out today."

"Well, Mr. Boyd," I said sincerely, "your future looks bright to me. Thank you for coming."

He stood with a grin, shoulders back, head erect, and walked to the door.

I stopped him. "One more question, if you don't mind."

Kaha'i turned to me.

"What could cause crustal displacement?"

"You mean what do I think? Personally?"

"Your opinion is the only one I've got."

He did his nervous tic shrug. "An outside force would be necessary. Something really big."

I pushed. "Like maybe a comet . . . or a rogue planet?" *Like, maybe Nibiru?*

He crammed his hands into his pockets and lowered his head. "I don't know."

"Do you have a theory?"

"No," he mumbled. "I'm just a student." We said good-bye, and he left before returning immediately to poke his head back in my doorway.

"Dr. Howard?"

"Yes, Mr. Boyd."

"You might like to know that positive magnetic energy has shown up in the South Pole area where only negative energy should be. So some kind of pole shift has already started."

He shuffled away, shrinking into the hunched geology student who had walked into my office half an hour earlier.

I stared at the empty door where Kaha'i had stood moments before. Maybe we'd be lucky and have a slow magnetic pole shift that would only kill fish, wheat, and trees. Much better than a crustal displacement, which, in Hovard's words, would destroy two-thirds of all life. After that, most survivors would starve. Reviewing the two scenarios, I realized both kinds of pole shift would create famine for survivors.

Resting my left arm on the desk, I turned it over to study the jaguar. The creature's dark, snarling profile with protruding fangs mirrored my mood. I'd reached maximum with the Mayan assignment, ready to do anything and be done with it. Maybe I could try a national advertising campaign. Reaching for the yellow pages, I turned to a long list of topics: Agencies, Direct mail, Electronic and Fax, Internet and Online, Newspaper and Shoppers Guide. A smile tweaked my mouth at the thought of an ad in Shopper's Guide.

Warning! A disaster is coming
Don't know what, where, or when.
Can't stop it.
Consider yourself warned.

I called the Monte Hales Creative Advertising Company. With a name like Monte, the guy had to work harder.

"This is Monte."

I used my professional tone. "I'd like to place a national advertisement."

"What did you have in mind?" I heard the anxious hunger in his voice.

"How much is a TV spot?"

"Depends on your audience," he said. "If you want an ad during the Superbowl, a thirty second spot costs two and a half million dollars. It goes down from there but not much." My intake of breath traveled through the air to his ears, so he modified his approach. "Take my advice and start advertising locally. If that goes well, you can expand to national." He was still happily hungry.

I lowered my expectations. "How about radio?"

"Fifty thousand bucks can get you thirty seconds at two stations for a couple of weeks. What's your product?"

"Uh . . . Public Service. How about magazines?"

His voice dove into disappointment. He couldn't buy a sweatshirt from the proceeds of my phone call. "One ad in one magazine, $2,000. I take it your finances are limited. Maybe you could consider the Web market, which is about a thousand bucks a month."

"You mean those annoying pop-up things that everybody erases without reading?"

"The very same."

"How about direct mail?"

"Lady, unless you're a congressman with franking privileges, the postage alone will put you out of business."

We ended the conversation, both of us thwarted. I couldn't

even afford a pop-up warning on the Internet. All the avenues folded in on themselves, rolling me back to square one. My resolve compressed into a black hole, and I stared at the dead-end wall in front of me.

A sharp stab in my memory told me to look at the clock. In five minutes, my pottery dating class was scheduled to take its final exam. Using language I'd heard from construction workers, I rummaged for the papers that should have been on my desk, neatly stacked and organized. Peering over the edge of oak, I saw them scattered across the floor where I'd dumped them to make room for the geology map.

I hated what the jaguar did to my life.

Not only that, I'd forgotten to ask Dr. Spokes about thermo-luminescence and stone tools for my article.

SEVENTEEN

During final exams I obsessed over the Mayan warning and how to deliver it. At night I dreamed of flying through the sky with a megaphone to announce danger. In real life, my assistants graded papers, leaving me free to brood over elusive problems, like the jaguar on my arm that wouldn't fade. Finally, I realized I couldn't warn anybody, but I would at least prepare my own little family.

The yellow pages had a heading titled, "Food Products, Wholesale," which turned out to be frozen stuff for restaurants. I searched the Internet under a variety of listings, finally hitting on "Preparedness and Survival Foods."

Bingo.

The topics were endless: dehydrated food, freeze-dried packages, three-day kits, stoves, storage. It was all there—an entire, expensive industry to serve the needs of paranoid people who believe the end of the world is coming. A bare bones list for one adult per year included foods I didn't recognize much less know how to eat. But storage for decades—with no rotation, except the water and oil—sounded attractive.

Grains . . . . 400 lbs.
Legumes . . . . 60 lbs.
Powdered Milk . . . . 16 lbs.

Oil . . . . 10 qts.

Honey/Sugar . . . . 60 lbs.

Salt . . . . 8 lbs.

Water . . . . .14 gallons

(a two week supply if you don't flush the toilet with it)

The dismal list left me questioning the value of survival. But the thought of watching Marisa starve encouraged me to enter a food warehouse that carried bulk items sealed in plastic buckets. When Marisa came home from school, she caught me lugging one of a dozen containers of wheat into the front room. She held the handle with me as we huffed into the house.

"What *is* this stuff?" Her eyes bored into mine, demanding answers.

I gave her the short version. "Wheat."

We returned to the car for another bucket as she asked, "What's it for?"

I grunted as I lifted the forty-pound weight, replying, "To eat."

We stacked the buckets three high to make a four-foot tower and then trudged to the car for more.

"I've never seen wheat before," she said as we struggled with a pail.

"It's hard brown seeds," I explained, "and it lasts for years and years."

Marisa's face screwed itself into revulsion. "I'm not going to eat brown seeds."

"Not now," I soothed her. "Later. Much later. Or never, that would be good too. But it will be here if later becomes now." *Very cryptic.*

Marisa dropped her half of the load inside the entry and crossed her arms. "I won't move until I know what you're doing."

The time has come to talk of other things.

Surrounded by white plastic buckets full of brown seeds, I told Marisa how I had accidentally taken an astronomer's place in Mexico, was drugged, tattooed, and told to warn my people of a massive destruction in the near future.

Marisa actually grinned at me. "I thought you'd had that ugly picture dug into your skin on purpose. I didn't ask about it because I didn't want to embarrass you."

I filled with love for the child-woman before me. "I thought I did a good job hiding it."

Marisa took a crooked stance, hand on hip, head cocked. "Come on, Mom. It's an animal head on the inside of your arm. You can't hide something that disgusting."

We talked. I told her everything, right up to Planet X. When I finished, she was all business. "Who are you supposed to warn?"

"I'm not sure. I think it might be everybody in the country."

"Maybe it's just us, your family."

I shook my head. "I think it's bigger."

"Have you warned anybody yet?"

"Yes . . . you. One down, millions to go. I haven't figured out how to tell them."

"Why don't you tell the government and let them take care of it?"

This is not the time to talk about government underground cities. "In a really big disaster," I said, searching for the right words, "the electricity will be out, telephones down. It'll be better if everybody can take care of themselves."

Marisa chewed on the idea for awhile and then posed her next question. "Do *you* believe there's a big disaster coming?"

I leaned against a tower of buckets. "It's taken almost a year to be convinced. Every time I put it aside, new evidence pops up. So . . ." I waved my arm to include the survival food, "Congratulations. You're the first person prepared."

Marisa nodded, as if agreeing on which movie to see. We walked back to the car and pulled another heavy container from the trunk. "What about," she began, "old Mrs. Evans down the street? Shouldn't we warn her?"

"Maybe we can store a little extra for her." We shared the

weight of the bucket back to the house with Marisa still deep in thought. "There's a single mom with three kids at the end of the block. We should store for them too."

The pail thudded on the carpet when we dropped it. The word *exponential* came to mind, as in, hungry people increase exponentially. "We can't feed everybody."

"They'll find out we have food." She looked around at the white buckets. "Even though it's nasty stuff. They'll take it from us. We'd better warn our neighborhood."

"Everybody will think we're crazy." The word *we* prompted me to stare at Marisa for a few seconds, trying to read her gullibility factor. "Do you believe me?"

"Not really," she said in a grown-up thirteen-year-old way. "But you've had almost a year to get used to the idea. I've only had ten minutes."

I hugged her. The kid was a born survivor.

We hauled the remaining buckets into the house and drove off for another load. When I had a hundred dollars left in the bank, we dragged ourselves home and collapsed.

Marisa incorporated the buckets into the house as part of the furniture. She arranged them two high with a round board on top to make a table. Fifteen took the place of a bed frame. She made bookshelves for her room. Chinese ingenuity.

Meanwhile, my dream about flying through the air with a megaphone haunted me.

EIGHTEEN

05.13.2005

No more school
No more books
No more teachers' dirty looks.

The words of the children's rhyme echoed in my head as the semester ended. Teaching a summer session wasn't an option. I needed to be with Marisa. But the China trip had devoured our savings, and the food storage flattened the cash in the bank. We looked for ways to earn money and still be together. I asked my department head to tell me if anything came in, checked the boards, and skimmed professional ads.

Finally, I called the director of a prehistoric Indian ruin outside of Flagstaff, called Elden Pueblo. They hired me to supervise student excavations while teaching research techniques and artifact analysis. Marisa would join the youth volunteers. We stuffed our old truck with the tipi, attached our tiny travel trailer, named *the Burro*, and made the two-hour drive.

Elden Pueblo scattered itself over several acres of Ponderosa Pines towering above the crumbling walls of eighty houses, a community room, and two kivas. The first excavation in 1926 yielded 2,500 artifacts, and the site was still going strong, offering a certification field school and public volunteer program.

We parked our fiberglass minitrailer in a primitive camp-ground and set up the tipi for additional space. Motels were avail-able in town, but we wanted to keep all our Forest Service salary. After getting familiar with the free chemical toilets and solar showers, routine took over.

On an evening during the first week, Marisa and I turned to our battery-operated radio to quell boredom. It spewed out a night talk show, bounced to us from San Francisco.

"Hello, Bill, you're on the air."

"I just want everybody out there to know that John Titor is real."

"You mean the time traveler from 2036?"

"That's the guy. Titor found the IBM computer he needed to take back to the future and he left."

The host exhibited massive control and respect for the caller. "What I don't understand, Bill, is why the future would need one of our old IBM's. If they've mastered time travel, they could make their own computer."

Bill gave a confident answer. "John Titor said it was a top secret mission. When we get to 2036, we'll find out."

"Well, the nation has your message, Bill. Thanks."

We stared at each other before breaking into peals of laughter and then listened for more mirth and merriment. A guy dubbing himself "Draco" was already busy educating everybody.

" . . . need to know that the government can create disasters using a weather experiment called 'The Haarp Project.' "

"Does that mean something?"

"High Frequency Active Auroral Research Program." The man's tone turned secretive. "You don't really think that big tsu-nami last December was natural, do you? The government did it."

"Why would the government create a tsunami in Indonesia?"

"Because they can."

"Uh . . . Okay then. Thanks for the call."

Anyone could freely say their piece. The radio show was worth the battery power we were using to listen. A movie in town couldn't have been more entertaining.

The first field school at Elden Pueblo registered forty-two students. In three weeks of digging they found two Macaw skeletons from Mexico, shell jewelry from California, and pottery shards made by Mogollon Indians from Texas. The place had been a central trading area. Marisa joined me in the evenings, covered with dirt and radiant about her volunteer work.

On June 12 my university boss called on my cell. I like Arnold Frederick. He's a black-and-white kind of guy while I wander into gray, but we get along fine as long as I don't tell him what my dark side is thinking.

"Hey, Arnold. What's up?"

He must have heard the sound of shovels in the background. "Are you at home?"

"I'm at a site in northern Arizona, outside Flagstaff."

Arnold didn't waste time with niceties. "We've had a request for an off-the-wall assignment in New Mexico. It fits your weird interests."

So much for my hidden dark side. I felt like a vampire when I said, "Which of my many bizarre tastes will this mission satisfy?"

He didn't take the bait. "A photographer went to Chaco Canyon in New Mexico, climbed Fajada Butte looking for petroglyphs, and claims there's an ancient calendar on top probably left by the Anasazi Indians."

The word *calendar* poked my interest awake. "Did you get a description?"

"Something about the solstice sun and a dagger of light shining through rocks onto a spiral. I didn't pay attention."

"You don't think that's exciting?"

"Primitive natives a thousand years ago," he patiently explained, "didn't need to figure out the longest day of the year by tracking the summer solstice."

"Come on, Arnold, you've seen what the Anasazi were capable

of. They built thirty-foot-wide roads spreading a hundred miles in all directions. At its height, their civilization was almost the size of Ireland. There's nothing primitive about Anasazi architecture, so why limit their astronomy?"

Arnold used his patient-parent tone. "Be logical, Matt. Indians didn't even have writing. They couldn't have worked out the solstice. If there's a calendar on top of Fajada, I'd sooner believe aliens from outer space left it there." I didn't respond to his insanity, so he continued, "I think it's a natural phenomenon, but the photographer wants scientists to see it at noon on June 21, when the sun creates the dagger. That's the date if you want it."

"I don't want it." My words were abrupt. "It's busy here."

A short pause hit my ear before Arnold spoke again. "Did I mention that the photographer has connections? There's a hefty grant that will pay for three specialists to analyze the site."

The guy had funding. Oh, the injustice. It just went to show, once again, that it isn't what you know but who you know that counts. At the mention of money my interest rose like a rocket. Arnold gave me contact information and wished me luck, which I'd need. In Chaco Canyon, June 21 would herald summer, meaning there would be hot winds, sticky skin, and no shade. Worse, while everybody else marked the solstice at sunrise, the Fajada event apparently happened during the blast furnace of noon. Maybe Arnold was right—my interests are weird. My need for money, however, is perfectly normal.

In my own little tipi, I made a call to someone named Soter. A woman's voice answered, and I shot to the point, introducing myself, profession, and university, asking for Mr. Soter.

"I'm Anna Soter," she said, her voice gentle, sounding young. "I made the discovery four years ago. It's taken this long to get funding for an official investigation." She told me the team would meet June 20 at Gallo Campground, climb the Butte the next morning to catch the show at noon, and then assess the data. I accepted her offer. With my antique one-person Burro trailer and a thirty-year-old truck to haul it, I could evade anything nature spit at me. I'd leave the tipi for

Marisa, who would be safely covered in dirt by day and guarded by friends at night.

A week later the old Burro and I headed for New Mexico. In the old days, the trailer had sheltered me and my little dog. Later it held me and my little girl. This time, I drove alone. Bone-jarring dirt roads pushed me around like a bully during recess, but it could have been worse. The maps warned that, "The route can vary from very rough to impassable." If it rained, the road would swallow my little rig whole. Finally, signs for "Chaco Culture National Park" directed me to the entrance. Gallo Campground sat a mile east of the visitor center, situated in beige dirt, sprinkled with khaki sagebrush, set against sun-faded cliffs sweating rust. I rolled into one of the forty-seven sites in gratitude. There were flushing toilets. Life was good.

In the early evening, a knock reverberated against my aluminum door. I called to the person to move away so I could kick the door open, and before me stood a young woman, perhaps in her early thirties, with straight brown hair curving on her shoulders. She wore light brown pants and a collared green shirt tucked in at the waist. Her face was slightly longer than normal, making her mouth seem lower than the classic beauty queen image. She had probably cried about it as a teenager.

"I'm looking for Dr. Howard."

"You've found her. Come in."

The girl swung into my tiny space. "I've never seen a trailer this small."

"My tipi is bigger," I informed her, motioning to a spot on the bed for her to sit, "but I left it behind for my daughter to live in."

She nodded vacantly, obviously not sure if I was joking but not willing to ask. Then she introduced herself. "I'm Anna Soter. Thank you for coming."

"It sounds like you've stumbled onto something unique."

"I hope so," she said. "After finding the solstice marker I took an archaeoastronomy class to learn more. The professor was excited when he saw my photos of the sun dagger and helped me apply for funding. He arranged for professionals to evaluate the place." *So the professor's reputation got us here.*

"I assume," I said, "we'll all meet tomorrow."

"Six in the morning at my place, number twenty. Get some sleep." She stood and reached for the door handle, but I stopped her. "Allow me," I offered and then did the necessary hand and foot dance that forced the door open. She deftly jumped to the ground and waved good-bye. There were ten extra pounds on her hips, but she moved like an athlete with confidence.

That night I listened to a national talk show out of Milwaukee, vaguely wondering how many of these things bounced along the airwaves of America.

"Welcome to the show, Gary from Omaha. What's on your mind?"

"I was taken aboard an alien spacecraft when I was six years old. They implanted a chip into the back of my arm. I wonder if anybody out there has had the same experience and if they got a doctor to remove it."

"Have you gone to a doctor?"

"No. He'll think I'm crazy."

"Have the aliens used the chip to control you in any way?"

"Not that I've noticed."

"Does the chip hurt?"

"I can't feel it, but it bugs me to know it's there."

The host politely backed away. "So, folks, if any of you have been chipped or marked and know a solution, give us a call here at . . ."

"There's no solution, Gary from Omaha," I grumbled to the radio. "A doctor can't remove it. You and your chip, me with my mark—we're both destined for doom."

The desert wafted its heat from the day's collection into the night sky, leaving only bitter cold behind. Around two in the morning, the wind started howling through the canyon walls like a pack of wolves, twisting around corners, spinning past boulders, rocking my tin tipi like a flood of water pushing against the aluminum frame. I felt sorry for the people camped in tents, trying to keep the fabric pegged to the ground. When morning dawned, the canyon slept, exhausted from its tantrum the night before.

NINETEEN

Chaco stands at 6200 feet, and the weather can vary sixty degrees. I prepared for both heat and cold, lowered myself from the trailer, and walked through morning air that was so still I felt my intrusion like a swimmer in tranquil water. Three people already sat at the picnic table in lot 20. I joined them.

"Welcome to Hell," said the man with a wiry, scruffy beard sitting across from me. He offered his hand, deeply tanned like the rest of him. "I'm Richard Manley, pressed into service as the geologist on this trip."

I noted the man's negative tone and wondered if he'd lost his tent in the wind. "I'm Matt Howard," I responded, "the archaeologist who volunteered to be here. After last night I'm questioning my sanity." I turned to the man next to me. "And you are?"

He was slightly built, clean shaven, with skin the color of rising bread dough. He obviously didn't spend time in the sun. "I'm Ralph Finlayson, physicist." He shook my hand weakly. "I'm supposed to analyze how the placement of the rocks force the sunlight against a carved spiral. My opinion is, it's lunacy to think Indians moved huge rocks to create a dagger of light on the summer solstice."

"The lunacy," Dr. Manley cut in, "is in us, coming here to

see an ordinary spiral petroglyph. No scientist would take this seriously."

"Somebody," I reminded them, "thinks it has merit. Anna has funding."

Dr. Manley's mouth tightened before he said, "Money talks louder than common sense."

An old colorless station wagon, caked with layers of the soil that surrounded us, stopped at our table. Anna emerged, wearing the same brown pants and tucked-in shirt I had seen her in last night. From the passenger side stepped a young man, his burnished skin stretched tight over high cheekbones, black hair held in a ponytail behind his neck. He wore levis and a long-sleeved blue shirt, a maroon cotton bandanna around his neck. I guessed he was Pueblo Indian or maybe Hopi. Both tribes claim descent from the Anasazi, which disappeared about AD 1300.

"This is Littlebird," Anna said. "He'll help us up the Butte."

With our introductions done, we climbed into the station wagon and headed south along the sand-filled road. Expectations and instructions passed among us, but soon silence accentuated the tires grinding against rocks, slipping into ruts. I watched the landscape roll by, like a theme park ride with boulders stacked precariously, ready to drop on squealing patrons.

We topped a rise to see Fajada Butte splashed in the gold glory of sunrise, a solitary sentinel on a vast, empty plain, waiting for eternity to end.

"Well, it's impressive," Dr. Manley said. "I'll give it that."

Anna smiled as if the geologist had complimented her child. "It's almost five hundred feet high," she proudly said. "The spiral calendar is on a ledge just below the plateau."

"I assumed it would be on the flat top," I commented, "to catch the sun."

Anna shook her head. "It's hidden so well, I still can't believe I found it." She parked at the side of the road, and we slithered into our packs to follow Littlebird across the uneven desert floor.

The Butte rose before us like a ziggurat, debris at its base rising halfway up the sides, as if ancient teenage stonemasons had left their work without cleaning up the mess. Loose rocks, pebbles, and boulders hindered our way, forcing us to scramble on our hands and knees. We finally stopped at a large, ragged fissure ripping through the rock.

"This chimney," Littlebird explained, "is the only way to the top. Follow where I put my feet. When it gets steep, we'll rope up."

If this isn't steep, I thought, *I'm gonna hate what is.*

We formed a line, Littlebird followed by Anna, the geologist in front of me, and then the physicist last. "Watch for rattle-snakes," Littlebird called behind him. "You'll be fine as long as you don't step on them."

"Terrific advice," the physicist mumbled behind me. "The park service should get rid of dangerous snakes."

"This is snake country," I flung over my shoulder. "We're the intruders here." I felt his animosity at the back of my neck. Finlayson and I were already bumping egos.

The sounds of sliding rocks and grunting climbers took the place of grumbling. Coiled snakes lay motionless in shade and crevices. We watched Littlebird climb higher, ropes hanging from his shoulders, banging against his back. Finally, we faced a sheer, vertical chimney. Handing his pack to Anna, Littlebird put the ropes on his chest, placed his back against one wall, feet pushing on the opposite, and shimmied up the chimney to stand on the ridge. Using himself for leverage, he put one end of the rope behind his waist. He dropped the other end to Anna, who tied it to her waist and imitated his horizontal scoot. Then they lowered the rope to haul our gear up.

"What's in this thing?" Littlebird joked. "Rocks? Heavy lead?"

"I've got measuring equipment," Manley yelled up, "and a few books."

"I'll send you the chiropractor's bill," the Indian hollered back. "Watch your heads. Down rope."

Manley tied the rope around his waist and worked his way up the mountain. When it was my turn, I followed his example, body taut between the walls, feet inching up, back scraping against the mountain to keep gravity balanced. I was grateful for the rope between me and empty air. When Finlayson joined the group, we clambered across the loose rubble below Fajada's summit, moving toward three upright rock slabs. They were eight to ten feet tall, leaning against the cliff with narrow gaps between them. It could have been a natural formation, unusual but not worth examining.

"This is it," Anna announced. We shuffled carefully on the ledge, aware of the four-hundred-foot drop to the desert floor. Reaching the monoliths, we peered through their gaps to see two spirals carved into the back wall behind the slabs, one about the size of a large dinner plate. The other, up and to the left, was half that size.

The scientists went into action. Finlayson opened his pack to begin measuring the gaps. Manley checked the rocks for content. I crawled behind the slabs to examine the spirals, entering the small alcove like a child in a cave, with the spirals on my right and the great stones leaning over my head like a roof. I analyzed the pecked carving, counted the rings in the spirals, and searched the rocks for markings.

Dr. Finlayson's voice filtered through the gaps as he offered his professional opinion. "Well," he began, "I think we can solve one problem immediately." He used an authoritative tone, the one I use with undergraduate students. "These slabs must weigh two tons each, placed on a precarious downward slope to a sheer drop. Nobody could move them here." He emphasized the word *nobody*. "Certainly not a thousand years ago. Not even today." He amended his statement. "Maybe a military helicopter could lower them into place, but I'd hate to be the pilot."

I crawled from the little cave in back, thinking of the words my own department head had used: *I'd sooner believe aliens from outer space left it there.*

"Maybe space aliens did it," I suggested. Too bad I didn't keep my thoughts in my head where they belonged. I'd just made an enemy of the physicist, who leaped into combat mode.

"You've been in the heat too long, Dr. Howard."

Before my quick wit made things worse, Manley, who had been examining the composition of the rock, added his take on the site. "I'm prepared to give my professional opinion. These rocks are natural, not carved or otherwise altered." He cranked his neck to check the cliff above the rock arrangement. "They could have slipped from above."

I'd been squinting at the top edges of the slabs. "Those marks at the top," I said, "could be from pecking and grinding."

Manley took the comment as a challenge. "I'll be glad to climb up there and prove there's no 'pecking and grinding' at the top." He grabbed the center monolith, swinging his left leg over the edge, and began scaling the ancient rock with his heavy hiking boots, disregarding the possibility of authenticity before we'd even analyzed the evidence.

"Are you crazy?" I moved to his side, placing my hand next to his lower foot. "You're going to—" *ruin, destroy, deface a priceless artifact . . .* "—kill yourself. If the rock shifts, you'll plummet over the precipice." My apparent concern for his safety slowed him, or at least activated his common sense.

A quiet voice entered the scene. "Dr. Manley." It was Littlebird. "I have a question about the cliff face over there. I wonder if you'd come and explain it to me." Manley slid from the center slab and followed Littlebird up the slope, their voices dropping away. *Fortuitous coincidence*, I thought. *Calamity defused.*

I revisited the diminutive cave behind the slabs to inspect the spirals again. The large one held . . . something I once knew in a former life but had forgotten. *Why didn't they carve concentric circles, like a bull's-eye? What's the purpose of the spiral?* I stared, waiting for truth to speak. It didn't.

"It's time," Anna called. "Everybody come back." We emerged from our various places of study. Littlebird and Manley sauntered down the slope, still talking. When the five of us gathered, Anna explained, "The show lasts about eighteen minutes. We need to place ourselves at the other side of the rocks to see the dagger without blocking the sun." She led the team to my little cave, which sheltered the spirals. We maneuvered ourselves into uncomfortable positions so everyone had a view.

At noon, a spot of light appeared at the top of the big spiral. It spread downward, forming the image of a dagger made of light. The morphing, moving light rolled across ridges and valleys of the carved spiral, exactly piercing the center. I heard a small gasp, whether from me or someone else I couldn't tell. Mesmerized, we watched the dagger pierce the bottom of the spiral to linger in a sliver of radiance before diminishing to a spot. When the light left the stage, an audible exhale escaped from the group. Apparently we had hardly breathed during the eighteen-minute display, perhaps thinking our movement might break and shatter the light.

Anna broke the spell. "It was an accident the first day I saw the sun dagger. If Littlebird hadn't stopped here to rest, we would have gone past." *The Indian was here from the beginning.*

"I hate to rain on the pageant," Finlayson said, "but the dagger isn't exclusive to the solstice. It probably measures noon every day."

I couldn't resist challenging him. "The Anasazi didn't need to climb Fajada to figure out it was noon. They could stay on the canyon floor and look at the sun."

"My point exactly," he argued. "The Indians didn't construct this, the slabs fell from the cliff above—"

I interrupted. "And just happened to land vertically, with openings to create sun daggers on the summer solstice." Sarcasm rarely works, but I use it anyway . . . can't help myself.

"Excuse me," Finlayson shot back, ignoring me and appealing to the rest of the group. "I have to remind you people that Indians weren't capable of hauling these slabs into place. This solstice light show is a freakin' fluke of nature. We'll have to return another day to see if the solstice marking is exclusive."

Manley and Littlebird remained quiet. Anna had maintained an objective face during our debate, but I saw her eyes cloud at Finlayson's last comment. "Littlebird and I have returned several times," she said. "The dagger makes its precise visual image only on the solstices, June 21 and December 21. My professor accepted the summer solstice measurement and developed a theory about the small spiral. At his suggestion, I returned to check it out."

She waited for heightened suspense.

"The dagger," she said, "moves directly through the center of the small circle at the spring and fall equinoxes." The group seemed too shocked to argue. Anna's smile framed her face in delight. She left the overhang and moved outside to the cliff face as we followed.

A sudden glimmer of possibility, a hunch maybe, or inspiration, called me back to the spirals. I slipped away from the group to crawl into the shelter, its shade a pleasant respite.

Anna's voice slid through the narrow slats of the giant blocks of rock. "At the equinox, the light goes through this gap to produce the dagger in the little spiral. Not only that, but two daggers—"

Finlayson cut her off. "I understand your need to validate this find, but no one in the ancient world measured both the solstice and the equinox. Ask the archaeologist."

"Dr. Howard," Anna said. "What's your opinion?"

I wasn't there, of course. I still hunkered in front of the large spiral, counting its rings again and smiling broadly at my new revelation.

"Dr. Howard? Where are you?"

I froze in my huddle, hoping they'd go away but knowing they wouldn't. "Behind the slabs," I called.

The group closed in. Manley finally spoke.

"What are you doing, Dr. Howard?"

"I'm in here contemplating the big spiral and counting its rings."

"Do I dare ask why?"

"There are nineteen rings, ten on the left, nine on the right. That's not a coincidence."

Finlayson's head poked into my space. "What's the significance." It wasn't a question, just a disgusted comment.

I crawled from under the ledge like a bug. "The moon has a

nineteen year cycle. Maybe our uneducated Anasazi also used a lunar measurement in their calendar." I looked across the desert to the horizon, imagining the moonrise lighting half the spiral.

Finlayson wasn't impressed. "Dr. Howard, surely you know that ancient people didn't measure equinoxes *and* solstices together in one calendar. They most certainly didn't include moon cycles."

He was right, so I avoided a direct answer. "Gentlemen," I proclaimed. "We may have the only place in the world that measures everything." I turned to Anna. "What else were you going to say?"

The girl's eyes sparkled with gratitude. "Furthermore," she picked up the dropped threads of her thoughts, "during the winter solstice, two daggers of light actually frame the large spiral." Anna tried to contain her excitement but couldn't quite accomplish it. "So we've got a twelve-month solar calendar measuring equinoxes and solstices and a nineteen year lunar calendar."

"Dr. Manley," the physicist appealed with annoyance, "please shed a little genuine science on this."

Manley steadied himself against a monolith with his chin raised to appraise the cliff wall rising to Fajada's summit. His next statement was spoken quietly. "These slabs came from further up the slope, where Littlebird took me. The striations match. They were carved from the cliff face. Somebody else will have to figure out how they were moved here and positioned."

"It's physically impossible," the pasty-faced Finlayson asserted.

I couldn't resist baiting him. "I guess the Anasazi didn't know that, since they moved the stones anyway."

Finlayson sputtered his frustration. "This is madness."

Littlebird's voice hovered over us. "There's a storm coming. We have to get off the Butte."

We looked up at the perfectly blue sky. "It looks good to me," Manley said.

Littlebird pointed to a swarm of ants scurrying into cracks. "Not to them. We leave now."

The trip off the mountain was done in silence. Littlebird and
Anna belayed us and the packs down the steep part of the chimney. During my turn, my back slipped, which caused my feet
to lose their position. For a few seconds I hung loosely from the
rope, wildly kicking, while everyone yelled instructions. Then
Littlebird climbed down, feet spread against the cliff sides for
support, to rearrange me. My left arm reached high to grasp the
rope, and his eyes caught the jaguar tattoo. Even in our risky
position, he stared and then looked at me and nodded, as if a
message had passed between us.

The remainder of the passage down Fajada went without
incident.

Moments before reaching our car, the sky opened to pour out
its entire water storage. We were soaked within three seconds. I
opened the car door to get inside but felt a hand on my shoulder.
It was Littlebird. I turned, a waterfall cascading off my nose.

"Dr. Howard?" I could barely hear him in the noise.

"Yes," I yelled.

"We've been waiting for you."

TWENTY

We could have been driving under a lake. Our windshield wipers vainly sloshed back and forth against the glass. I took deep breaths to assure myself there was air in the car. The downpour rattled the roof of the station wagon as Anna crept through ruts in the road-turned-river. Half the precipitation in Chaco comes from sudden, intense rains, creating flash floods off the slick rock. Anciently, Chacoans captured runoff in stone-lined irrigation ditches, channeled to their fields on the canyon floor. Now, however, the water fled to places that produced nothing.

Anna coaxed the car to the top of a rise and stopped, waiting for a break in the weather. When the rain ceased, it was so abrupt we wondered if the experience had been an illusion, but hot mist rising into the air confirmed it. We moved again, cautiously traversing the muck as we congratulated Littlebird on getting us off the mountain and asked how he knew.

"My people," he explained, "are taught by our fellow desert creatures. We study them on earth and in air. My ancestors once used the sky to track time." He held up his wrist and smiled. "Today we use watches."

"It's lucky," Manley said, "that Littlebird showed me the cliff shelf. There's no question the monoliths originated there and were moved to the site. We all witnessed the summer solstice. Precise measurements for the equinoxes will have to be verified later."

"I already have four years invested in this," Anna said. "I'm willing to spend more."

This seemed a good place for my contribution. "I still say there's pecking and grinding on top of the blocks to create the slivers of light. If so, the Anasazi had even more skill than we thought."

Finlayson looked thoughtful. "You may be right." I was shocked to hear the physicist agree with me as he extended the logic. "A curve at the top would be necessary to create the dagger effect."

My opinion of him morphed into admiration. The guy could alter his opinion when forced to by facts. "Dr. Finlayson," I said with new respect. "Some of us won't live long enough to check out the moon connection. Would you design a lab experiment based on a model of Fajada Butte to check a nineteen-year lunar calendar?"

He actually grinned, his bread-dough skin creasing at the corners of his mouth. "I'll get one of my slaves to do it. Or maybe a graduate student . . . same thing."

We laughed amiably.

Anna dropped everyone off at their campsites, reserving me for last. Littlebird personally carried my pack to the trailer door.

"I'll pick you up at four o'clock."

I looked at my watch. "That's in an hour," I protested.

"Four in the morning," he corrected. The kid actually suggested four in the morning without muscle twitches or eye twinkles. He was dead serious.

"Where did you say we were going?" I asked as he handed me the backpack.

"I didn't," he whispered. "We cannot discuss it here. Say nothing to anyone." He nodded politely and returned to the car, now an anemic brown from the mud. I could have said no. I should have. But the Indian had likely saved my life on the mountain. Anyway, heightened intrigue had a stronger pull than good judgment.

The team ate dinner together, sharing measurements and opinions. Littlebird was absent, no doubt arranging something awkward for me. Anna, thrilled at the outcome of our petulant beginning, grilled steaks and listened to us laugh. Sometimes scientists are almost as good as real people.

It was 10 PM when I forced my way into my tinsel teardrop trailer and crashed on the mattress that also served as seating for the table.

Littlebird came early. A light tap on the metal door disturbed my nightmare about being lost in a giant refrigerator, searching for a coat and boots. Then a louder knock woke me fully to face a reality which was, in fact, cold. Rolling off the mattress, I dressed as someone thumped on my shaded glass window.

"Right," I called out. "My eyes are open." Working socks over my feet before slipping into shoes, I moved to my cup-sized sink to brush my teeth while the knocking returned to insistent tapping. I grabbed a coat, warned, "Get away from the door," and then kicked it open.

"Nice door," the Indian said, both hands held up in a sign of defeat.

"It's exactly the way I want it," I declared. "Nobody can get in."

"My truck is designed for security too," he said, leading me to the passenger side of a vehicle that might have been red beneath the dust. The layers of sand couldn't hide the dents and crunches along its body. He balled his fist and hit the door four inches left of the handle. It opened smoothly to let me crawl onto the cracked plastic seat cover. The young man slammed the door viciously behind me and it clicked into place. He moved to the driver's side.

"I love this truck," he commented, sliding behind the wheel. "It always starts." The engine choked, sputtered, coughed, gave a raucous backfire, and rolled to the dirt road, where we turned right.

From the window I saw my own reflection against the dark night. I turned to Littlebird, studying his classic profile before saying, "Well, Littlebird, I don't know what this is about, but I trust you, so I'm going."

The young, tanned face wrinkled slightly in a puzzled expression. "You don't know? Didn't you come here to meet with us?"

"What makes you think that?"

"You carry the mark."

"Oh, *that*." I settled my spine into the plastic upholstery, producing a sound like crinkling paper. "This tattoo has caused me nothing but trouble. It was intended for a man I know, an astronomer."

He nodded a little. "I have to admit, we were expecting a man."

"Believe me, I wish you'd gotten him."

Littlebird ignored the sarcasm. "How did you get the mark?"

"I went to Chichen Itza and accidentally took the man's place. They dragged me through a ceremony, and I woke up with a jaguar on the inside of my arm." I leaned forward to look at him and accent the words, "I tried to have it removed."

The waiting time between my statement and his response became uncomfortable. He finally spoke. "It won't come off."

I heaved an audible sigh and stared out the window again. "That's what the astronomer said." Turning my head, I asked, "Would you like to take me back and wait for the right person?"

He concentrated on the two circles of light illuminating the road. "Maybe you're not the right person, but you're the *only* person. There will not be another."

"How do you know?"

"The prophecy is clear. When the marked one comes to us, we are to give him . . ." he looked at me and then returned his eyes to the road, " . . . or her . . . the warning prophecies given to the Old Ones."

"But I'm a mistake."

Littlebird began the phrase I hated to hear. "There are—"

"No," I stopped him. "Don't tell me there are no mistakes."

I'd always believed Indians don't guffaw, but this one did. The wretched kid laughed out loud. "Dr. Howard, I was going to say there *are* mistakes, the world is full of them, but the Universal Father has power to take our blunders and work them for good."

"Well then," I stated flatly, "we're stuck with each other. Where are we going?"

"To the kiva."

"Which one? There are probably a thousand here in Chaco Canyon." *Everywhere, close together, next to each other, kivas on top of kivas . . . underground ceremonial centers where the men of a tribe met.*

"This is a working kiva, not on the Park Service maps."

A twinge of anticipation entered my archaeologist's heart at the opportunity to witness a functional kiva, but I knew the rules. "You might not have noticed, since I'm getting old, but I'm female. I can't enter your kiva."

"We are Hopi," he replied evenly. "Male and female work as one. The ancient Hisatsinom believed the Great Father blessed all His children equally with knowledge."

"Hisatsinom? Should I know that word?"

"It's a Hopi word for the people of long ago. You call them Anasazi, a Navaho word meaning ancient enemy. We hate the name."

"I'm sorry. I wish I could fix it, but 'Anasazi' is the assigned name and isn't likely to change, even if you request it."

Littlebird spoke without rancor in a matter-of-fact tone. "We stopped asking your scientists to listen to us. They poke into our history, come to wrong conclusions, and publish their errors. You should know the correct name, *Hisatsinom,* because you must learn our prophecies to warn your people."

I inhaled deeply, closing my eyes in frustration. *How am I supposed to warn anybody?* Exhaling stress, I let it join the dust on the dashboard. "Start at the beginning," I said, resigning myself to my fate.

We drove past Chetro Ketl and its huge kiva while Littlebird told me of the great teacher who had visited the Hisatsinom, showing them ways of peace and leaving prophecies of the future.

I like time lines and inquired, "When did this happen?"

"So long ago we can't translate it on our watches." I said nothing. He continued. "The Hopi believe there have been four ages of Man." *Mayans have five ages,* I thought, *but four is close enough among friends.* "The end of our current cycle," he said, "will have three great shakings to warn us that the time is near. The first two shakings were less powerful, with only one hand." *Were? They've already happened?* "The third will be done with both hands. Our instructions were to give the warning to the people in the great glass house after the second shaking. In 1959 we sent a delegation to the United Nations but were denied permission to speak."

"Back up," I requested. "I thought the shakings were earthquakes, but now it sounds like something else. What are you talking about?"

"Just listen." It was a command. "Before the earliest shaking, the prophecy described carriages first pulled by animals and then suddenly moving by themselves. Some carriages, with smoke coming from the top, would connect in a line on an iron road. Black ribbons would crisscross the land for carriages to follow. People could speak into cobwebs covering the world and be heard everywhere. Finally, carriages would fly in the sky. Then the first shaking happened."

"The shakings are . . ." I halted.

"World Wars," Littlebird finished for me.

We drove past the sign for Pueblo Bonito, highlighted briefly by the headlights of the truck. I thought the kiva might be there, since there are at least forty at the Great House. But we bumped past as I asked, "What were the signs of the second shaking?"

"Before the second shaking, a people would rise to power who were governed by the mirror image of our peace sign."

The mirror image of . . . I sat straight in shock. "The swastika,"

I blurted. "I've seen the reverse swastika all over the ancient world. It symbolized peace."

He nodded. "Our universal peace sign was turned backwards as a war symbol. We were told the people of the swastika would join with people of the rising sun. Another nation would invent a gourd of ashes and drop it from the sky to end the second shaking."

"The atomic bomb," I spoke to myself. Littlebird's jaw tightened as he heard the words. Suddenly, without slowing, he swerved off the road into a canyon wash, and the truck floor ground over what sounded like a small boulder. He turned the wheel sharply, striking a dirt hump. I hit my nose against the window. Bright sparkling lights flooded into my brain, and pain clouded my vision. Littlebird struggled to regain control.

"Sorry," he apologized. "I was thinking of atomic bombs, not paying attention to the turnoff. We'll be there soon."

"Tell me what to expect at the kiva, so I don't embarrass you."

"This is a sacred ceremony."

"I haven't had a lot of luck at sacred ceremonies. You won't draw blood, will you?"

"Not this time," he replied, grinning enough for me to see. Then he became serious. "Answer questions but don't ask any. You're not a curious archaeologist tonight. Don't look around at pictures, don't count pillars, don't fidget. Listen to what the elders say as if many lives depend on you, because they do."

We ground to a halt on the gravel in front of a four-foot-high wall. Littlebird pushed the gear forward, stepped on a brake pedal, killed the lights, pulled the key, and then exited the car to move to my side. When he hit the door, it swung open, and he helped me out into the cold. We walked to the truck bed for a package containing two wool blankets and a pair of leather moccasins. As I changed shoes and wrapped the blanket around my shoulders, Littlebird caught a glimpse of my face.

"Are you bleeding?"

"Could be," I said. "I hit my nose pretty hard." I reached up to check for blood, but he grabbed my hand.

"Don't touch it. It's a sign."

This "sign" stuff is getting silly. "Gimme a break," I said. "It's just a bloody nose."

He seemed almost excited, as if my particular nose held the answer to his doubts. "It is blood sacrifice. You are acceptable." I searched his face for a glimmer of humor, but there wasn't any.

"Fine," I murmured. "Anything to be acceptable."

We walked to the wall, which curved into the dark. "By the way," Littlebird used a low voice. "If you tell anyone about the kiva, we'll have to kill you."

"What?" My tone squeaked.

He shushed me and said, "Let's make this easy. Answer all questions with 'yes.' Don't do anything else. I'll seat you where you need to be. Don't tell anyone where the kiva is."

"I couldn't find this place again if my life depended on it."

"It does. Keep bleeding."

TWENTY-ONE

We walked on a wood platform leading to an opening in the ground. I expected to use a ladder to enter the kiva, but there were steps disappearing into a dark hole. I turned to my companion/guide and whispered, "Would you really kill me?"

He stood behind me, holding my elbow for balance on the first stair. "Don't test it," he hissed.

We descended. As we did so, I thought I could make out some details in the wood of the fourth stair. The seventh was illuminated by a flickering glow. We stepped past a door frame shaped like a "T" and continued to the twelfth step. A short wall before us acted as a foil for the only source of light: a raised fire pit in the center of the room. Six square pillars, painted bright red, held the roof in place. Trees that large must have come from forests miles away. I didn't dare crank my neck far enough to study the ceiling, but it rose higher than I had anticipated from my studies of ruined kivas—perhaps eight feet. Without moving my head, as per instructions, I estimated the room at a thirty foot diameter. Barely discernible in the shadows was the expected bench circling the periphery. The round wall above it, painted white and decorated with colorful designs, reminded me of the caves of Lascaux or carvings at Ireland's Newgrange. The pictures seemed alive, jumping under the wavering fireli—

Littlebird crunched my elbow harder than necessary, reminding me not to ogle the kiva. He seated me opposite the fire and stairwell, modified my position a little to the right, and then faded into the shadows. Weird kid. I adjusted my blanket, sat still against the kiva wall, and waited.

And waited.

As my eyes adjusted to the dark, large bundles appeared on the bench, forming into people wrapped in blankets. I couldn't count them without turning my head, but the faces I could see, diffused between light and dark, showed only stoic disinterest. Some wore a headdress similar to earmuffs . . . like Princess Leia in *Star* . . . no . . . like the hairdo Hopi women wear. I maintained an emotionless façade but grinned broadly on the inside, knowing I had sisters here.

Smoke lazily rose and disappeared. Since the kiva was free of haze, I assumed there was a hole in the roof. A slight draft of air brushed across my face. They had an air shaft for ventilation. It took great self-control not to search for it or at least count the number of people, but I held firm.

I began to think the entire ceremony was a test of calcified calm to see who would break first. Then a deep male voice spoke, the surprise of it made my gut tighten.

"You carry the mark?" His voice was low, like the chief in Disney's *Peter Pan*.

"Yes," I answered in a confident tone.

"You will show the Council." *Not a question . . . does it require a yes?* I decided no comment was a good comment and unburied my left arm from the blanket, lifting it to show the jaguar profile, fangs protruding. Nobody "oooohed" or "ahhhhhed," which was disappointing.

"You will keep the sacred covenant and never disclose what you see here today."

What if there's human sacrifice? I'd have to report . . . "Uh . . . yes."

"Hear now the Hopi Prophecies before the Third Shaking."

There was a short silence until a new voice, male, began speaking. "An eagle will fly into the sky and land on the moon."

An older woman's voice, cracking at the edges: "Men will become women, and women will change into men."

Another voice, female, younger: "Morality will be gone. The sacredness of the family will be destroyed."

A man: "The white man's government will be completely corrupt."

A voice so old it was genderless gave the next prophecy: "Man will find the blueprint of life and begin making animals."

A woman: "Schools will be an enemy of the people. Teachers will change history and traditions."

I stopped keeping track of the male/female voices to focus my attention on their words. How could I remember it all? I tried an old memory trick using visual pictures pegged to each other: a giant eagle on the moon holding a cross-dressed couple in his beak. The woman-made-man holds a picture of a family torn in half. The picture floats to the ground, turning over to show the American flag, also torn. A sheep, representing man's attempt to make animals, eats the picture while school children . . .

The people surrounding me continued the prophecies.

"There will be a great commotion in nature: hurricanes, floods; the seasons will change until a farmer can hardly tell when to plant seed. These changes are because Mother Earth is trying to rid herself of the sins of the people."

"Time will speed up."

"There will be a house thrown into the sky. Men will live in it. The house will fall and look like a blue star."

"A great famine will occur as part of the Third Shaking. Tell your people to store food for at least three seasons."

"The bear and yellow people with a red flag will attack this country."

"An alignment of the planets is a sign that the Third Shaking is soon."

"The nation that dropped the gourd of ashes to stop the

Second Shaking will have a gourd of ashes dropped on them at the Third Shaking."

They stopped. The kiva sat in cool stillness. A breeze tickled my face—the only movement in the round room. Then the chief's deep voice rumbled through it again.

"These are the Hopi prophecies. Do you have a question?"

Littlebird said the correct answer would always be yes. Did I have a question? Absolutely, positively, and I wanted an answer.

I belted out a resounding "Yes!" like the beginning of a song. No one gave me permission to speak, but they didn't shut me up either, so I forged ahead. "I think you're not telling me everything."

A shock wave bounced around the walls for a couple of seconds before it settled. After several moments of profound silence, the chief must have motioned for someone to speak their lines because a new voice answered my question.

"We find your people cannot hear the true end of the last cycle. They are uncomfortable with Spirit. But you have requested it. During the war in this country, a small group from the west will rise, fight, and win, though death will be heavy. Those who survive will welcome the People of Light who come to help restore a new society of peace based on freedom. They will go throughout the world to bring those who desire peace to join us in this country. The day will be glorious. Blades of grass will erupt through the earth to see that day. Energy will come from the magnetic field of the earth, new construction patterns will be introduced. We have sad days ahead, ending in greatness."

The Chief spoke. "There is wisdom in not giving this prophecy to a people who cannot receive it. Later is time enough. Now, your people must prepare to survive, so the great day will shine on their children, who will begin a new golden age."

There was stillness, the kind that honors something.

"Dr. Howard," Littlebird's voice broke the quiet. "It is time."

Nobody moved. I took my cues from the group and stayed glued to the slightly off-center position Littlebird had placed me in. Once, I almost stood to say, "Well, it was nice meeting you," but I didn't. I sat there until a small round spot of light shone on the center of the glowing fire pit. The Hopi began a soft chant as the light moved slowly through the fire and across the floor toward me, like the sun dagger on Fajada, growing in size until it reached my moccasin shoes. It traveled like a living thing, wiggling up my legs to become a blinding pillar of light from chest to head. I closed my eyes against the brightness as the warm light penetrated my skin to fill the spaces of my existence. It passed leisurely from the crown of my head, and I imagined a sliver of light on the wall behind me, slipping into nothingness.

The kiva turned dark again. "You," the deep voice said, rich and soothing, "take the light to your people."

The Hopi stood as one, climbing single-file up the stairway. I remained seated, not knowing what action to take. When the kiva was empty, Littlebird led me to the opposite side of the fire pit. He placed a gourd of water in my hands and motioned for me to pour it on the fire. Steam filled the room like a sacred mist, cleansing the kiva and blessing its ceremony. We mounted the stairs to emerge alone into the desert day.

I shattered the spirit as we walked to the truck. "Where *is* everybody?"

"They park closer to the road to keep this spot sacred."

"Why did *we* get to park here?"

He squirmed. "They heard you were . . . uh . . . an older woman and thought the stairs were all you could handle."

I laughed loud enough to scare every lizard within a twenty-yard radius. Littlebird whacked on his car door, slid me inside, and we peeled out, spreading road dust over everything.

The Indian handed me a tissue to wipe the blood off my face. "So?" I asked him, rubbing under my sacrificial nose. "How did I do?"

"That depends on whether you can remember the prophecies."

I spouted them off like a recording, explaining my picture sequences.

He shook his head. "Wouldn't it be less complicated to just memorize?"

"I beg your pardon," I said as if insulted. "I cheated my way through graduate school with this system. Today wasn't the time to try something new." As we drove, I grew serious, a rare occurrence. "How do I spread the news?"

"Well," Littlebird offered, "we've already tried and failed at the United Nations, so that saves you a step. You'll have to do something else to get people to listen."

"What if I fail?"

"You're not responsible if no one believes you. Your job is to warn; theirs is to accept. Destiny finds those who listen. Fate finds the rest."

We drove in silence as I observed the changing desert colors and cliffs highlighted by the sun. After a few minutes of considering the last two days, I had questions.

"Did you lead Anna to the spirals four years ago?"

"Yes. I thought Anna would be the messenger, but the elders waited for a man who carried the mark."

I laughed. "So they ended up with a tattooed lady." I caught sight of the jaguar peeking out from its hiding place under my sleeve. Suddenly Sumerian legends, Mayan calendars, the Chinese *I Ching*, and Hopi predictions linked arms like old friends. They joined with my jaguar—symbol of the Fifth Age and the jaguar prophecies.

We bumped along in silence for a while, until I thought of another question.

"The sun dagger in the kiva hit me precisely. How did you know where to seat me?"

"Yesterday was the solstice, so I figured it would be off a little today."

The kid had guessed—nothing ethereal, spiritual, or ghostly had directed him.

I moved to the next question. "How many people were in the kiva?"

"Thirty-six. Most Hopi live on three mesas in Arizona, so

some of them traveled a long way to give the warning for your people."

"Why do the Hopi care about my people?"

"Frankly, we don't. But the Great Father does."

I considered the importance of the Hopi message. "If you were taking this warning to your people," I asked Littlebird, "what would you focus on?"

He didn't have to think. The response rumbled into the air. "Famine."

That comment shut me up, and we drove through the dirt without dialogue. When we reached my petite trailer, Littlebird escorted me to the door, handing me the blanket and moccasins as souvenirs.

"I just have one more question," I said.

"Anything."

"Would you really kill me if I talked about the kiva?"

"Of course not."

"That's a relief."

"But we'd have to track you down and beat you to a bloody pulp." He grinned.

Nice.

TWENTY-TWO

My meeting the next afternoon with Anna Soter and the other scientists went late, forcing me to drive the route to Elden Pueblo in the dark. Drowsy, I hit the radio button.

"Welcome to . . ."

Yawn.

" . . . nationwide audience . . . fifteen million listeners . . ."

I twisted my neck, sending crackles along the tendons, and reached for a chocolate covered pretzel.

" . . . we have a guy from Denver who wants to be anonymous."

The caller had an "uh" complex. "Uh . . . I don't want anyone to . . . uh . . . recognize me. I'm an ordinary guy who . . . uh . . . knows some real scary stuff about the . . . uh . . . Denver International Airport."

"Your call is confidential. What's your scoop?"

"Uh . . . space aliens have built a huge . . . uh . . . underground city beneath the airport. I caught a glimpse . . ."

"It's not space aliens," I said to the radio. "It's the government."

Suddenly awake, I wrenched the wheel toward the lip of the dirt road and slammed my foot against the brake pedal.

176

The words *national audience* and *fifteen million listeners* had finally caught up to my bleary brain and now they blinked like neon lights behind my forehead. I nearly ripped my shoulder out of its socket trying to wrestle my bag from the floor and find my cell phone.

"Come on, come on," I commanded the radio, "announce your toll-free number."

The subject of lizard people beneath the Denver Airport went on for a few more minutes before it died and the number was offered.

I dialed it.

The woman who answered wanted to know my name, where I was calling from, and, of course, my alias. She put me on hold, and I waited in the dark desert, rehearsing words.

There was no heads up before I was on the air.

"Hello, Jaguar Lady," the male voice said. "You must have something important on your mind to be calling in the middle of a desert between New Mexico and Arizona."

I lowered my voice a few notches to give extra authority and disguise my identity. "I'm a scientist and university professor. It's vital that people hear this message. The planet is in danger from several sources." I said the words unemotionally and in a straightforward tone. "Massive destruction is coming. People need to prepare. The biggest . . ."

"Wait a minute, Jaguar Lady. Where are you getting this information?"

I considered my slim sources. "From archaeologists, astronomers, geologists, construction engineers, and even Mayan elders. Tell people to store food and water."

"When did you say this was coming?" The host didn't have a joking tone in his voice. Maybe he was taking my warning seriously.

"It isn't possible to predict dates," I returned. "Get long-term storage."

"Don't you think you're fear-mongering?"

"Being practical isn't fear. If I'm wrong, you'll end up with a lot of food around the house. If I'm right, you and your family might have a chance for survival. The stakes are worth the gamble."

"Are you serious about this?"

"Dead serious."

I led a double life at Elden Pueblo, examining pottery during the day, gathering data on a correlation between a shard's thickness and dates of production. At night I sneaked away to a private hill with good reception and became the Jaguar Lady, calling a different station each night.

I warned the nation about myriad misfortunes ahead of us: electromagnetic pulses from the center of the galaxy, solar storms that could fry us, and Planet X. "If you survive the disasters," I warned, "you'll face slow starvation. Get ready."

After three weeks, a woman called shortly after my performance on a station out of Milwaukee.

"Tell the dragon lady to shut up."

"You mean the Jaguar Lady?"

"Whatever. Her doom and gloom is tiresome. If the end of the world is coming, like she says, survivors will be in a scene from that terrible movie, *Mad Max*."

The host climbed aboard. "It won't be a scene," he said. "It'll be the whole lousy movie."

"Well, I'd rather die on the first round."

Thereafter, people lunged in line to demand public execution of the Jaguar Lady. I had failed again. Slipping from the national spotlight, I slithered back to full-time archaeologist, consoling myself with Littlebird's words: "Your job is to warn. Theirs is to accept."

I'd done all I could, but the jaguar still sat dark inside my arm. The assignment wasn't finished.

We returned home in August. Our Scottsdale house welcomed us, its desert landscape resembling twisted Play-Doh baking in the sun.

There were dishes in the sink, dead flies stuck to hardened food. The smell of mold wafted from the laundry room, where unwashed clothes waited. Every houseplant had withered into a zombie of its former self. The cactus in my home office still clung to life by the tips of its trembling little spikes. I apologized to the ugly thing and watered it.

08.05.2005

The to-do list said "pick up dry cleaning." I drove down the wrong street, did a partial U-turn, and came bumper to window with the second-hand shop owned by the classy little old lady with the gravel voice. I slipped into a parking space and entered the store. The bell was gone.

"Hello?" I preferred the bell.

A young girl in her twenties emerged from between the purple beads still covering the door to the stockroom. "May I help you?"

"I was expecting the older woman who works here. When will she be in?"

"She's dead." The girl folded her arms on the counter, waiting for my response. I didn't have one. My face must have looked stricken, because the girl softened and said, "Are you a relative?"

"No," I said, still in shock. I shook my head to clear it. "I'm not even a friend, never learned her name. I met her once, she said something that's still on my mind, and I came by to ask her questions. I'm so sorry I . . ." *How can I say this? Sorry I missed her? Sorry she died? Sorry I didn't get what I needed before the old gal kicked off?*

The girl leaned her head to one side and then new under-standing streamed into her face.

"Are you Matt Howard?"

It was my turn to be surprised. "How would you know that?"

"Hazel left a tape for you." *Her name was Hazel. I'll bet people called her "Hazey" as a nickname. It would fit.* The girl was still talking. "She made the tape before . . . you know . . . before her last trip to the hospital." We stared at each other, discomfort sparking between us. "Anyway," she added, "I'll get it for you."

The girl pushed her way through the beads, which produced a snapping sound as the strings swayed against each other. When she returned, she held a midsize manila envelope, my name scratched on it with a pen that had skipped. I took the thing reverently, then felt stupid for caring about someone I hardly knew and crammed it into my pack.

"Thank you," I said. "I'll take this home and listen to her . . ." *final words?* " . . . wisdom." *Yeah, that was good.*

At home the familiar treasures of my study wrapped me in a security blanket. Pictures of my life, works, and awards beamed at me from the walls. I moved the cactus aside and let the envelope rest against my monitor. So the classy little lady named Hazel had gone off and grated out her last breath.

For a moment I considered the brief journey of this life and the skewed priorities we spend our days on. Then I pulled myself together. We could all go crazy if we concentrated on the ways we waste our lives. I carefully pried apart the flap and withdrew the familiar purple paper, folded in half, cradling an old-fashioned cassette tape. It was lucky I still owned a relic that would play the thing.

I saw the quotes I'd read months earlier on the purple paper and then turned it over. There were six additional statements on the back, all predicting positive outcomes.

PROPHECIES OF THE END TIME OF OUR DAY

Nostradamus

At last the wolf, the lion, ox and ass,
The gentle doe, shall lie down with the mastiffs.
The manna shall no more fall to them,
There shall be no more watching and keeping of mastiffs.

Mother Shipton

Before the race is built anew,
a silver serpent comes to view
and spew out men of like unknown
to mingle with the earth now grown
cold from its heat, and these men can
enlighten the minds of future man
to intermingle and show them how
to live and love and thus endow
the children with the second sight,
a natural thing so that they might
grow graceful, humble and when they do
The golden age will start anew.

Mayan Priest Don Alejandro Cirilo Oxlaj Peres

The Vale of Tears, the Nine Hells, is over, and it is time to pre-
pare for the Age of the Thirteen Heavens. Let the dawn come. Let all
the people and all the creatures have peace, let all things live happily.
Now is the time to go out into the world and spread the light. Now
is the time that the prophecies will be fulfilled.

The Kolbrin Book of Manuscripts, chapter 3, part 1 from the Great Scrolls

In those days men will have the Great Book before them, wisdom
will be revealed . . . The dauntless ones will survive, the stouthearted
will not go down to destruction.

From the Hopi Prophecies

Those who survive will welcome the People of Light who come to help restore a new society of peace based on freedom. They will go throughout the world to bring those who desire peace to join us in this country. The day will be glorious. Blades of grass will erupt through the earth to see that day. Energy will come from the magnetic field of the earth, new construction patterns will be introduced. We have sad days ahead, ending in greatness.

Carlos Barrios and the Mayan elders

They say that the world will end in December, 2012. The Mayan elders are angry with this. The world will not end. It will be transformed. What is unfolding is in perfect order and the earth has seen it many times before.

All the prophets sang the Mayan theme song: "We've seen this change before." Setting the purple paper aside, I picked up the tape labeled, "To Matt Howard" and stuck it in my old Walkman player. A gravel voice filled the room.

"Hello, Dr. Howard. I hoped to see you again, but you didn't come back in time, so I've taped my two bits." I smiled at her old-fashioned term. She coughed long enough to make me nervous, even though I already knew the end result. She continued. "Humans are tough, resourceful, smart, and kind. You heard right, sweetie—we're kind. When the chips are down, people pull together. That's our best survival trick. Listen, my dear, here's what everybody needs to hear. Warn them to prepare, but mostly tell them not to be afraid. Our ancestors have survived these events many times before, and so will we. This is like having a baby. The process hurts like hell, but when it's over, you've got something worth having. After all, it's not the end of the world—close, but not the end." The little lady laughed hoarsely across time at her own joke. "I'm sorry I'm going to miss it. But I'm supposed to be here, you're supposed to be there. You know the saying . . . there are no mistakes."

The tape gave a click, ending in silence.

I stared ahead at my bulletin board, seeing only assorted documents stuck like bugs to the ragged brown cork. Gradually, my attention focused on a thin, gray piece of paper held up by a red thumbtack. I didn't remember putting it there. The invisible aura around it made me stiffen.

CHUN

_____ _____

_____

_____ _____

_____ _____

_____

Starting at the bottom, the hexagram told my life during the last year.

One: A difficult beginning. Do not push but do not give up. Accept help of Sage. *Hovard explained precession and the 2012 end date. Carlos showed me the calendar in the landscape of Izapa. I learned that December 21, 2012, is the merging event of the sun and Galactic Mother.*

Two: Solution present itself. Undesirable obligation created. Wait for solution, correct in every particular. *Do not become emotionally involved with a married man.*

Three: Bad feeling will make you want to give up work. Do not do. Bring great misfortune. *I gave up for a few months, but the Hopi Prophecies brought me back.*

Four: Dark will hide light. Go slow. Have method. Quiet balance. *In other words, don't jump into national talk shows until you know what to say.*

Five: Do not act alone. Seek advice of Sage. Be patient until path is clear. *Hovard is the Sage. I can't complete this assignment without him.*

Six: Unite if sincere. Sage will bring good fortune.
Eventually, you will have to work with Dr. Michael Hovard.

That night I dreamed Hovard flew through the air with a megaphone. The next morning I collected phone numbers of national talk radio shows and called Hovard's home. His wife answered.

"Hi, Lisa," I spoke brightly, as if we'd been friends for years. "This is Matt Howard from the university. We met at Christmas. Is Dr. Hovard around?"

Her sweet breathy voice said he was at his office.

Marching across campus, I passed the Foucault Pendulum without dawdling. The astronomer's door exuded an overwhelming presence, like its master. I knocked.

"Come," his voice called from the other side of the portal.

Swinging the door open, I stood within its casing. Hovard's face widened in surprise. He halfway stood, thought better of it, and lowered into his chair again. The space between us filled with electric anticipation.

"Hello, Michael," I quietly said. "It's time."

TWENTY-THREE

Hovard sat at his desk, staring alternately at me and the page of phone numbers I'd shoved at him.

"You did what?" He set the list aside.

"I called those numbers every night for weeks, warning about the end of the world, unloading everything from precession in the Mayan calendar to the Chinese *I Ching* and the Sumerian story of the returning star Nibiru, which I connected to Planet X."

Hovard groaned. "I told you not to do that."

So did the I Ching: *Do not act alone. Seek advice of Sage.*

Hindsight is worthless. I closed my eyes and shook my head, embarrassed at my foolishness. "Not only that," I confessed, "but I included sunspots and pole shifts and the Hopi prophecies about a third world war. Then I told them about EMP bombs that would destroy digital circuitry. Everybody hates me. I don't dare show up again."

"And you want me to . . . ?"

I pointed to the list in front of him. "Take over the radio talk shows. Be your charming, positive self. Tell people, in your professional announcer's voice, not to be afraid."

He grinned like a little boy. "You think I have a good voice?"

"Get real, Hovard. You sound like smooth oil on a baby's bottom. You were born to talk on the radio. Besides, you know all the answers."

He nodded agreement.

I avoided a comment on his vanity, instead giving unnecessary instructions based on my failure. "Focus on a pole shift because it covers almost everything that people need to prepare for. Don't add anything else to the mix unless a caller brings it up. Stay on the air to answer questions. Don't include the 2012 center date unless you're pushed. Most of all, don't cause panic." *Unlike me.*

"And," the astronomer said dryly, "while I'm on the radio fielding questions and being attacked . . . what did you say you'll be doing?"

"I'll be in charge of writing a small book and sending it free to whoever wants it."

"No," he spit the word through his mustache.

I borrowed the first line of an old pop song. "It's my party and I'll write if I want to."

Hovard leaned forward to emphasize his point. "There has to be a price, or people won't value it."

I sighed. The guy was always right. "Okay," I said, "enough to cover printing and postage."

"You need help writing it?"

My first impulse was a resounding no. I'm a published author—I don't need help. But he added the clincher. "It will be more impressive with two doctorates on it."

"I hadn't planned on giving my name," I said. "We could lose our jobs."

The confident astronomer shook his head slightly. "*Hamlet's Mill* couldn't have been published by a single author. Two scientists working together gave it power. They didn't get fired."

The argument had merit. "Okay," I agreed. "If you're willing to put your neck in a noose, I can swing too."

09.21.2005

We published five hundred copies of the book at an independent company. Thus prepared, Hovard made his coast to coast debut. I hovered near the radio.

"Welcome to the show, Dr. Hovard. You're an astrologer?"

"I'm an astronomer," Hovard corrected.

"What's the difference?"

"An astrologer is a fortune teller." I could hear the tension in his voice. "I'm a scientist and university professor who studies and maps the cosmos."

The host shifted into safety. "What's your message?"

"Your audience needs to know that the planet is preparing itself for a pole shift." Hovard's deep, melodious voice gave him immediate leverage. "Positive magnetic energy is forming at the south pole where only negative should be. This indicates that something is already happening."

The host cut in. "Maybe you should explain what a pole shift is."

Now Hovard could shine. "There are two kinds. The first is a crustal displacement when continents actually move, which is extremely rare if it exists at all. The second is a magnetic change, reversing south pole to north and vice versa. Ancient rocks show there have been hundreds of magnetic pole shifts, so it's nothing new." Nice, casual, nonthreatening information. I could have done that.

The host showed interest. "What happens in a magnetic pole shift?"

Hovard turned practical. "When you change polarity in an electric motor, it rotates in the opposite direction. That's what Earth could do, change the direction of its rotation, causing stress to the surface."

"Hold it." The host was hooked. "You mean Earth literally turns the opposite way?"

"That's what the rocks say."

The presenter probed. "What could cause that?"

"We're not sure. Earth's pole changes might be related to sunspot activity. The sun changes poles every eleven and a half years with its sunspot cycle. It's due for another switch in about the year 2012."

"Is that dangerous?"

"Not usually, but this time NASA predicts 50 percent stronger solar storms than we've ever seen before. It could push us into a pole shift of our own."

"You're saying it will happen in 2012?"

"No. I'm saying the sun is due for a pole reversal in 2012. There's no date for a pole shift on Earth. It could take a hundred years or happen overnight. This is uncharted territory. All we can do is advise people to prepare for a very long camp out."

"How many months should we plan on?"

"Not months. Years. Don't expect electricity, flushing toilets, or take-out anytime soon."

"Are you related to the Jaguar Lady?"

The wretch remembered me.

Hovard was quick. "I think some of the Jaguar Lady's bad news was true, but there's also good news. Energy from the Solar storm will reload Earth's battery to be stable again for thousands of years. We just need to be informed and plan to keep living." He gave a plug for the little book and was invited back as a guest the following week.

We ran out of books that night.

I was jealous.

Hovard repeated his performance every evening on a different station. Clueless people called in with vacuous questions.

"I don't see the big deal," a lady commented. "We'll just eat out until the emergency is over."

Hovard spoke gently. "What will you do when the restaurants run out of food?"

There was silence at the other end of the line.

"Hello?" The anchor said, "Are you still there?"

The woman's icy voice returned with an attitude, as if the answer should be obvious even to a couple of men. "Restaurants can't afford to run out of food," she said. "It would hurt their business."

The host was happy to let her go and move on to the next equally inane question, this one coming from a young man.

"I don't think people should hoard food," he said. "The government will give us what we need."

"I wouldn't count on that," Hovard replied. "The government traditionally takes care of itself." I sent frantic mental messages screaming not to get into politics. He would ruin everything.

"Don't you think," I heard his voice glide through the ether, "that your survival is too important to leave to anybody else?" I could have said it just as well. Maybe better.

A woman called in sometime during the second week.

"All the officials say people like you are nuts. If what you're telling us is true, the government would instruct us on what to do. NASA would tell us there's danger."

The air waves were empty for a long three seconds before Hovard spoke. "A natural disaster of Biblical proportions is forming." He used his lowest resonance for authority. "How would you announce that?" Pause. "You wouldn't. It's simple logistics. The government can't save three hundred million citizens in this country. They aren't going to help you."

When the woman spoke, her tone held uncertainty. "I'd at least give people a chance."

Hovard sealed his point. "The officials believe it's best to avoid panic as long as possible. I'm warning you because it's the right thing to do. You can act on it or not."

The lady turned timid. "How can we know what the truth is?"

Hovard was brutal. "You can't," he said. "Good luck."

A hostile man called in. "You're crazy, dude, telling me to buy several years' worth of food."

Hovard reacted calmly. "That's the practical solution."

"I've got a better idea," the lummox challenged. "If this disaster happens, and I'm still alive, I'll take my gun and help myself to food off the shelves."

The host cut in. "Trucks have to stock the stores daily. In a huge disaster, looters will empty the shelves in a few hours, and they'll have guns too. Expect riots, mobs, and shootings."

The caller considered the logic, composed himself, and resumed. "Okay, let's say I get supplies and then die in your disaster. All that money and effort is wasted."

Hovard took over. "Not wasted. Somebody else will use it."

"Why should I care about anybody else?"

"It's not anybody else," Hovard's velvet voice responded. "It's the human family. It's *your* family."

It was a brilliant answer, beyond my ability. I shed a few tears and ate an entire jar of Nutella.

TWENTY-FOUR

A few weeks later at breakfast, Marisa uttered words that deflated my face.

"There's a man on the nighttime radio," she remarked between slurps of cold cereal. "He's better than you were, not as scary."

I froze in midair between toast and jam to gather my wits. "What are you talking about?"

"When you were the Jaguar Lady, you talked about creepy stuff."

"How do you know I was the Jaguar Lady?"

My daughter shrugged her tiny shoulders. "At Elden Pueblo you left the tipi every night. I listened to the radio. Your voice sounded lower—nobody would know it was you." It took a nanosecond for Marisa to realize she'd hit a wound, and she hurried to soothe me. "You should be glad the other guy's doing it because he knows all the right things to say." I lifted my eyebrows at the insult. She changed tactics. "Is that the man who should have gone to Mexico instead of you?"

Straightening in my chair, I raised my arms like a frustrated referee calling a foul play. "I got his invitation by mistake! The mark should be inside *his* elbow." I pushed the cereal bowl aside, crossing my arms on the table. "I've lived in Gehenna all year so he could—"

"What's Gehenna?"

At the wise age of thirteen, Marisa rarely asked questions, so I took a break from my tirade to embrace this teaching opportunity. "Outside ancient Jerusalem there was a dreadful garbage dump in a deep, narrow valley called Gehenna. They even threw dead bodies of criminals and animals into it." Marisa's rapt attention encouraged me to grosser additions. "Maggots and bacteria caused a stink that reeked for miles. The mix was so lethal that fires would break out spontaneously."

Marisa's eyes widened. "See what I mean, Mom? You talk about creepy stuff." She grinned and added, "Keep going."

I fanned the fuel of my daughter's macabre delight. "They added brimstone to keep the fires going, which made the stench—

"What's brimstone?"

"It's sulphur. When you strike a match, you can smell it, sort of like rotten eggs." I stretched my arms on the table for emphasis, palms down. "Imagine a whole valley full of rotting bodies and sulphur fires."

Marisa spoke in awe. "And you *lived* there?"

She hadn't understood the metaphor. I turned my palms up in a gesture of explanation, baring the inside of my arms. "Not literally, Marisa. It's a symbol. 'Gehenna' is a term for hell. I feel like I've lived—"

"Mom?" Marisa's attention had locked on my left arm. "What's happening to your tattoo?"

I glanced at the inside of my elbow. The jaguar had faded to half its original brilliance.

Leaping from the table, I stared at the picture on my arm. Sudden anger shot the next words from my tongue. "Hovard is doing my job."

Rage forced me into physical movement, and I strode around the dining room.

"They lied to me," I fumed. "They said I was the *one*."

I whirled to face an alarmed Marisa. "I got the mark. The work was mine." Clearing the dishes, I grabbed milk, bowls, and utensils to slam in the kitchen sink. "Now Hovard gets the credit." Glasses violently joined the bowls. My rational mind registered broken glass. I ignored it, intent on wreaking vengeance like Planet X against Earth.

Marisa anxiously rose to protect the leftovers and me. "Why didn't you do it without him?"

I stopped moving. My DNA is genetically programmed to divert water away from my tear ducts, so I rarely cry. But Marisa had thrown a sneak pass. "I couldn't," I admitted. "Hovard knew more than I did. He spent years studying precession and the Mayan calendar." I brushed a tear from the side of my nose. "I needed him."

Marisa cleaned spilled milk from the table. "Could he do a good job on the radio without you?"

I sat at the empty table to consider. "No," I finally concluded. "I told him about underground shelters. I connected *Hamlet's Mill* to Planet X. It was me who saw the Galactic Center alignment at Izapa. I learned about the time wave of the *I Ching*."

Marisa gently guided me. "So he didn't know everything."

"He didn't connect Venus transits to disasters." I squared my shoulders. "He knew nothing of the Hopi prophecies or other world seers. I gave him the geographical pole shift results. I wrote the book that's being sent across the country, even though his name is also on it." I nodded at Marisa. "He needed me too. We had to do the job together."

I laughed at the sudden revelation. Raising my eyes to the ceiling, I said aloud, "There are no mistakes."

That afternoon, with new confidence, I ordered several thousand books to give away.

The radio interviews reached millions. Hovard refused television offers, preferring to remain faceless. Most other astronomers publicly ridiculed him, but some supported the campaign. He shouldered praise and pundits equally well.

I was invisible . . . like the jaguar tattoo—now a shadow of its former glory.

Lisa Hovard invited me to dinner one evening. Suspicion rolled off the candles. There were two conversations involved, one with words, another without.

Lisa: "Well, Dr. Howard, how long have you and Michael worked together?"

Translation: Are you having an affair with my husband?

Me: "It's been over a year. The project is almost finished. I'm sure you've discussed it with Dr. Hovard. You must be very proud of him."

Translation: Get real, sweetheart. I pride myself on good taste.

Michael (too quickly): "I don't think Lisa is interested in what we've been working on."

Translation: Everybody shut up.

Lisa (in a wounded tone directed at Michael): "I'm interested in why you're gone every night." She smiled slightly at me to soften the reproach. "It must be exciting work."

Translation: I'll get an explanation from Michael tonight.

Me: "It's been fascinating."

Michael (at the same moment): "It's too boring to discuss."

Clacking of forks, chewing of salad.

During the main course, Lisa and I compared motherhood experiences. She wanted to know more about adoption, and I asked for advice about teenagers. Over dessert, we laughed like old friends. When the evening finished, we made a lunch date. Michael sulked.

Hovard stopped calling the radio talk shows, but other people have taken his place to raise the warning. Large supermarkets now offer storage foods sealed in buckets and nonhybrid seeds in cans. Primitive survivalists teach classes on fire-making with bow drills, simple traps to catch small animals, and emergency shelters. You can even learn how to tan hides using the animal's brains. Reality TV features survival situations, showing how to find and cook grubs, insects, and spiders.

Television documentaries are deep into an overkill of the Mayan end date, never explaining that 2012 is the center of a seventy-two year zone in the galaxy we've already entered.

Hovard occasionally calls to discuss weird manuscripts not found on common library shelves. We still market our little book, which clarifies that, whether we have a pole shift or one of the myriad other scheduled events—and whether it occurs in 2012, 2046, or beyond—it's not the end of the world. It may be close, but it won't be the end. Humans survived in the past. We'll do it again. Make plans to live.

Destiny finds those who listen. Fate finds the rest.

And God said, Let there be lights in the firmament of the heaven to divide the day from the night; and let them be for signs, and for seasons, and for days, and years.

—Genesis 1:14

There have been and will be again many destructions of mankind . . . leaving only those of you who are destitute of letters and education; And so you have to begin all over again like children, knowing nothing of what happened in ancient times.

—Plato, in "Timaeus"

I didn't know how to tell you.
In the end, I followed the example of
our ancestors of the fourth age—
I told the truth in a story.

—Matt Howard
(Phyllis Gunderson)